FRIGHTMARES 3

EVEN MORE SCARY STORIES TO READ – IF YOU DARE

BY MICHAEL DAHL

ILLUSTRATED BY XAVIER BONET

STONE ARCH BOOKS
a capstone imprint

TABLE OF CONTENTS

SECTION 3: WATCH OUT!

Dear Reader,

One night, I stepped outside to get some fresh air. It was a dark, moonless December night in Minnesota. The winter had been warmer than average — no snow on the ground and leaves were still clinging to the trees.

Someone was standing across the street and appeared to be staring at me. The figure stood in the alley across from my house, next to a row of bushes. The figure was dark. I couldn't see its face or even the color of its clothes.

Silently, smoothly, the figure glided sideways, then disappeared behind the bushes. I rushed over to the alley (I know, bad idea), and in mere seconds the figure was gone. Vanished!

I KNOW WHAT I SAW, but I don't let it scare me.

Strange figures and shadows hide in the stories of this book, staring out at you.

Be brave — stare right back!

Michael Dahl

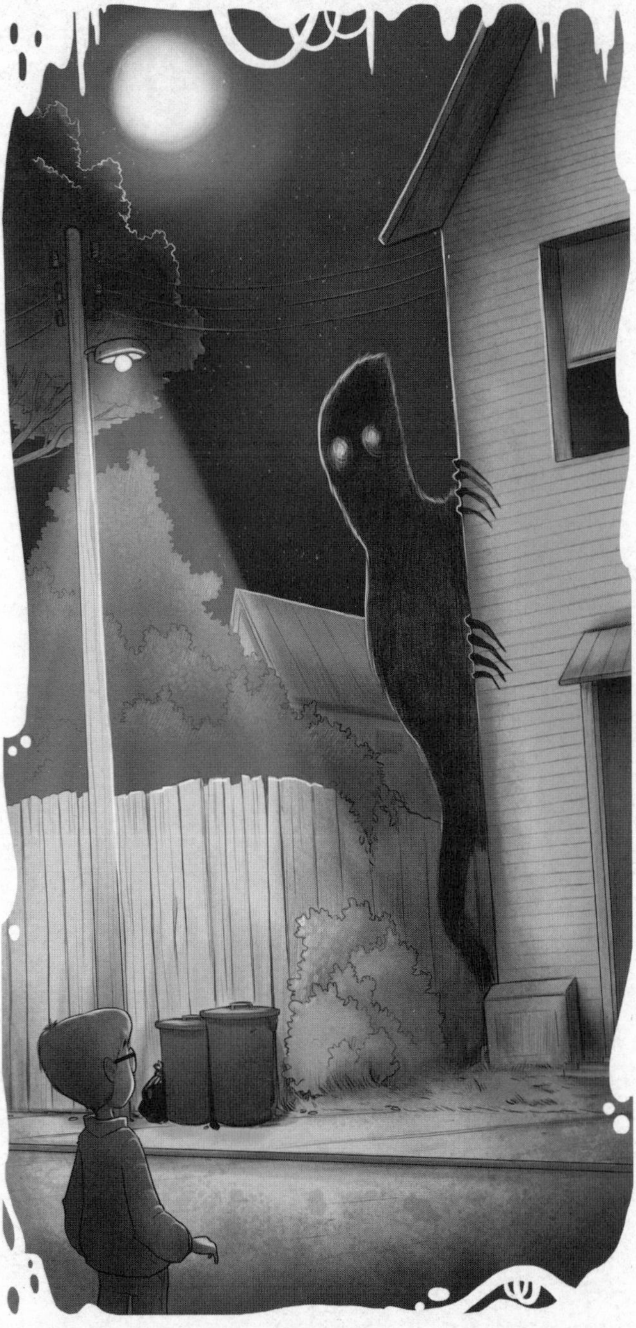

SECTION 1

IS ANYONE HOME?

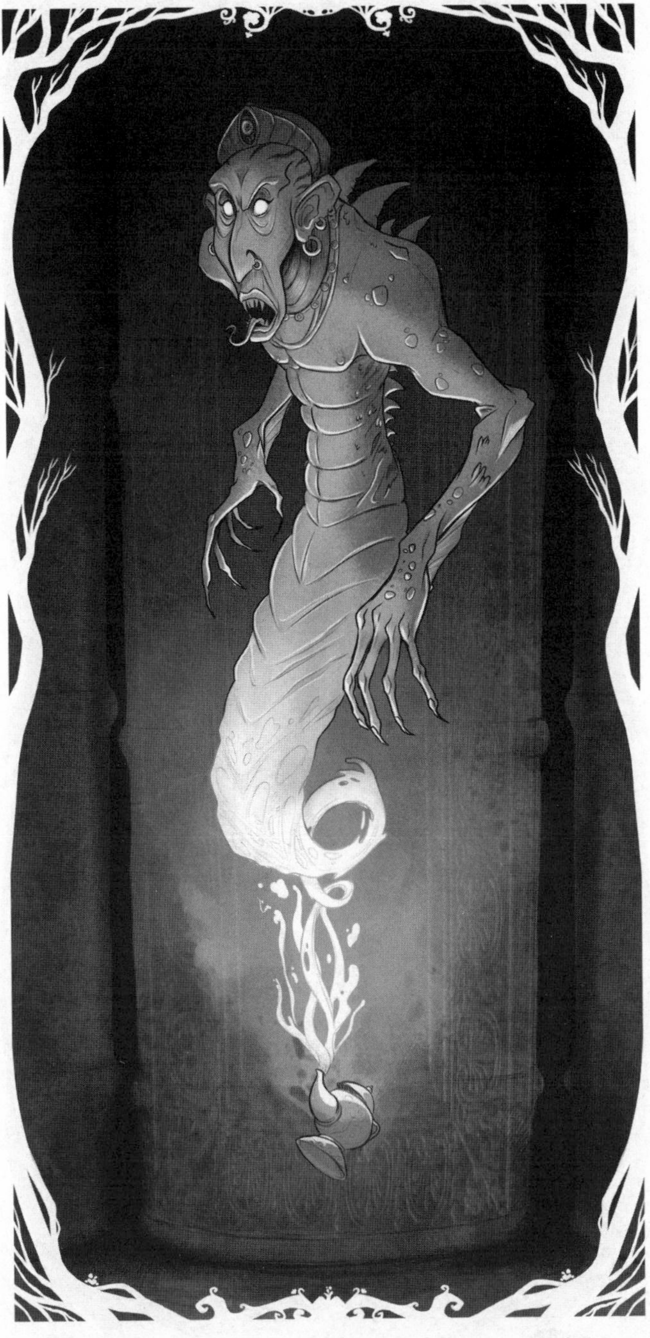

THE BOY IN THE BASEMENT

Ten-year-old Natalie stood at the top of the basement stairs. A single bulb hung above the last step. The rest of the basement remained in thick shadow.

Natalie gripped the banister. She took a few cautious steps down. Was that a moving shadow beyond the circle of light? Were her tired eyes playing tricks?

No, she told herself. *There's nothing there. Nothing. There.*

She backed up the steps and firmly closed the door.

When her family had first moved into the old house a few weeks ago, Natalie had found a piece of blue paper in her closet. The room had belonged to the girl who had lived here before. Natalie figured the paper must have belonged to the girl, something she had forgotten. She unfolded the paper and saw six words written in faint handwriting: *Feed the boy in the basement.*

Natalie's body had gone cold.

During that first week in the new house, she accompanied her father and her brothers, Mike and Kalen, when they carried boxes to store down there. The basement was old and had a cold stone floor. The brick walls were painted white. Old-fashioned lights hung from the ceiling, the kind that you switched on by pulling a small chain. Natalie was tall for her age, but she was still too short to reach the chains. She decided that first week she would never go downstairs alone.

Instead, each night at dinner, she would think of the message on the paper. *Feed the boy in the basement.*

After dinner, Natalie would open the door to the basement and stare down into the darkness. She didn't know why she did it. Maybe to prove to herself that the message had been a joke. It might have been part of a story the unknown girl had written.

No one could live in the basement, she told herself. Her parents or her brothers would have seen something.

* * *

Natalie's family had been living there for two weeks when she heard the noise. She had just gone to bed when she heard a creak. The basement door was opening.

Natalie shivered and snuggled into her bed. She heard the sound of footsteps walking across the kitchen floor. The footsteps stopped outside her door. *This can't be happening,* thought Natalie.

Something scratched on the door. Natalie felt like screaming, but she was too scared. She gripped the covers, her hands clammy with sweat, as her bedroom door slowly opened. A shadow stood there.

"Feed me. . . . ," it said.

Natalie screamed and shot under the covers.

Then she heard laughter. The light switched on. She looked up and saw her two brothers shaking with laughter.

"I knew that would get you," said Mike.

Natalie's face was red. "You two are super mean!" she said angrily.

"Mike found the note in your closet when we were moving boxes into your room," said Kalen, grinning. "He left it there, but then we thought it was the perfect prank."

"We weren't sure if you had read it or not," said Mike.

"Then we saw you looking down the basement stairs after dinner every night," said Kalen. "And we knew."

"It was perfect," said Mike. "Perfect."

Natalie jumped out of bed. "How do you know there *isn't* a boy in the basement?"

Mike rolled his eyes. "We've been down there a hundred times."

"So?" said Natalie.

"C'mon," said Kalen. "I'll show you."

The three siblings walked into the kitchen. Mike flipped the light switch. Kalen reached into the cookie jar on the counter and grabbed two chocolate chip cookies.

"Are you watching?" asked Kalen. He opened the basement door and hopped down the steps. Kalen looked up at the two of them.

Mike was still laughing. "Don't waste those cookies," he called down.

"Watch," Kalen said. He held the cookies like he would a Frisbee and tossed them both into a dark corner.

"Hope he likes them," said Mike.

Natalie leaned forward. She hadn't heard the sound of the cookies falling on the floor.

"He'd better," said Kalen. "It's Mom's recipe."

Kalen turned at a sound. From the top of the stairs, Natalie and Mike saw a long, slithery pink tongue shoot out of the shadows. It wrapped itself three or four times around Kalen, then pulled him into the dark.

There was a nasty smacking sound, followed by a low purr. Without meaning to, they had fed the boy in the basement.

SKIPPY

Dinner was not going well. Milo kept stealing glances at his mother and father, back and forth across the table, across the soup. His mother and father were not speaking. They hardly made any noise at all. They were too busy listening.

They were listening to sounds coming from the kitchen. Milo, however, ignored the moaning and the huffing. He ignored the churning sound of food spilling all over the tile floor. He ignored the *flip-flip-flop* of the dog's tail happily hitting the wall. It was a noisy reminder that Skippy had knocked over and broken seventeen separate items in the last week.

Milo's father set his spoon down, resting it against the rim of his soup bowl. He took a deep breath. "Skippy —" he began.

"Skippy is good!" Milo said. He was surprised that he spoke so suddenly, so loudly. His father was surprised too. He gave Milo the look he sometimes gave to his laptop when he was having computer problems.

His dad began again. "Skippy is —"

His mother interrupted. "Yes, dear, Skippy *is* a good dog. But he has problems."

A very gross sound came from the kitchen.

"Lots of problems," said his father.

Milo knew that his parents were right. One of Skippy's problems was hard to ignore. He would forget to bark at the back door so he could do his business outside. Little brown surprises appeared on rugs and carpets throughout the house.

"Did you know," Milo had said one day after school, "that in Paris they call dog poop *la chocolate*? We learned that in French class. So that means Skippy is trying to be nice and give us treats."

"Well, *la chocolate* belongs outside!" his father had said. "Not in the house."

No sense of humor, Milo had thought.

Sitting at the dinner table, Milo was hoping that Skippy had not left another treat in the kitchen.

It was his mom's turn to sigh. She looked at Milo's dad and said, "I think we should tell him."

"Tell him?" asked Milo. "Tell him what? I mean, tell *me* what?"

His dad pushed his chair away from the table. "As you know," he said, "Skippy is becoming more . . . challenging. He's making messes and biting. He's breaking things and running up and down the stairs —"

"But he doesn't always do bad things," said Milo.

"Maybe not," said his father. "But he is getting worse."

His mother frowned. "Skippy is just not working out."

"What do you mean?" said Milo. But he knew what they meant. It was happening again.

His mother looked at the kitchen clock. "Let's get it over with," she said.

Milo's father stood up and walked into the kitchen. His mother followed. Milo sat still. The same thing was happening that had happened to several of his former pets. He didn't want to watch. He stared at his soup. He was trying so hard to think of another solution and was wishing he were far away.

His mother stepped quickly back into the room. She stood behind Milo and said, "Don't come outside, dear. You might get struck or have something hit your head. You know how these things are. It's . . . it's easier this way." Then she was gone.

Milo heard the back door open and his parents walk outside. The moaning had stopped, and the boy no longer heard the *flip-flip-flop* of the dog's happy tail. He knew Skippy was with them.

Milo kept sitting. His parents would be walking through the backyard, getting farther away from the house now. They needed room.

Suddenly, Milo needed room. He couldn't breathe as he sat there, waiting. He jumped up from the table. He ran outside and saw his parents standing in the grass, his father holding the little, struggling dog.

"Milo!" shouted his mother.

"Go back in the house," his father ordered.

It was too late. It was happening. Milo heard the sound and looked up. There it was. Like a fat black spider, a delivery drone from the pet hub hovered. It buzzed like a wasp as it eased down to the ground. Its six thin arms held a box.

Milo stood back. Drones didn't always slow down in time to make their landing. Sometimes their arms twitched and boxes fell out of the sky. He had a friend whose family had ordered a new refrigerator. It had landed on their car.

This drone flew smoothly. Skippy would soon be sailing back to the pet hub. The hub's popular return policy said if there was any error with one of their robot forever friends, they would take it back. No questions asked. Full refund. Milo knew that his father would place Skippy inside the box, snap the lid shut, and watch the drone carry Skippy back to the factory.

Milo's family had bad luck with pets. The cuddly black kitten named Pouncer spit electrical sparks when it purred. The lop-eared rabbit drilled through walls. The cinnamon-colored pug had a weight issue. It floated at random moments throughout the house, bumping against the ceiling, breaking lamps, drifting through cobwebs. Milo had thought it was cool having a flying pet, but his parents were having none of it.

His father thought their house was too close to the power lines. His mother, who watched a lot of horror films, suggested that ghosts were playing tricks on them.

Milo didn't know what the problem was, he just knew he was never going to have a pet like his friends did. He walked slowly back toward the house and heard the bark behind him. That wasn't Skippy's bark. Skippy was already on his way back to the store.

"Milo," said his mother.

The boy turned and ran to his parents. His father was holding a dog — a different dog. The dog was small and brown and squirmy. "It's alive!" exclaimed Milo. He held out his arms and took the puppy from his father. "It's a real live dog," he said.

His mother smiled. "We knew how much you wanted a pet," she said. "And the robots were just not working out."

"But live ones are so expensive," said Milo.

His father was smiling too. "Not a problem, son," he said.

Milo nuzzled the puppy as he carried it toward the house.

His mother looked fondly at the boy. She noticed that his left leg kept swinging out at an odd angle. His head rotated once on his shoulders, then adjusted itself. His left ear made a popping sound and fell off as the boy closed the door behind him. *More Milo problems,* thought his mother.

She looked at her husband and said, "I think we should tell him."

He nodded. "I'll call the factory in the morning."

SHADOW SHOES

Daphne was too old to still believe there were monsters under her bed. But for the past three nights, she'd heard noises down there. Bumps and thumps, as if something had been dropped onto the wooden floor. She was convinced it wasn't an alligator or a zombie, but that still didn't make her brave enough to peer under the bed.

Whenever she heard the noise, Daphne checked the clock on her nightstand. The glowing numerals always displayed 10:01.

One night, before Daphne turned out her light, she set her alarm clock to ring a few minutes before ten o'clock. When she awoke, she lay in bed. She pulled the covers up to her chin and waited for the noise. If nothing happened, she'd know it had been a dream. Slowly the minutes passed, then . . .

Thump! Whump!

It was not a dream. Daphne reached over carefully and turned her light on. She slowly slid her legs over the side of the bed, and her bare feet slipped down to the cold wood floor. She sat on the edge of the bed for a full minute.

This is stupid, she told herself. *There are no monsters under the bed!*

Daphne knelt down and lifted the covers that draped from her bed to have a look.

She gasped. She never expected this: a pair of shoes. Shoes that were not hers. Daphne pulled them out for a closer look.

Even though Daphne's bedside light was on, it was hard to see the shoes. They appeared fuzzy, as if her eyes were still sleepy. Their shape reminded her of running shoes. It was hard to make out their color, but Daphne guessed they were a deep midnight blue. Her favorite color. Pale, glowing stars decorated the sides of each shoe.

Most importantly, they looked exactly her size.

Daphne sat on the edge of the bed and tried them on. Why not? Maybe her mom and dad had put them there as some kind of early birthday present.

When Daphne slipped them on, she felt relaxed. The shoes fit perfectly. Even without socks on, they felt warm and soft. Now she could see the shoes clearly. They were indeed a lovely shade of midnight blue, with twinkling stars on the sides. And as the stars pulsed with a glowing orange and gold, the bedside light went out.

Daphne didn't care. She could still see by the pale light of the stars.

She had never owned a pair of shoes this comfortable before. The strangely wonderful feeling traveled through her feet and legs and into the rest of her body.

Daphne stood up and took a few steps. She stepped into a rectangle of moonlight at the window. Suddenly, Daphne had an urge to walk outside. She ran into the hallway — then quickly stopped. She looked back at her bedroom door. It was closed. She hadn't touched it as she had raced into the hall. How did she get out here?

Daphne reached for the doorknob. The tips of her fingers felt a strange coolness, but that was all. Her fingers seemed to pass through the knob, as if it were only a shadow.

Some people might feel frightened by that. Daphne was thrilled. She ran downstairs, the shoes barely making a whisper on the steps. When she got to the back door, Daphne reached out. Again, her hand passed through the knob. She took a deep breath and made a bold decision.

She closed her eyes and walked forward. In a few seconds, she felt cold air brushing against her body. Daphne opened her eyes and found she was standing outside in the alleyway, just a few feet from her back door.

Daphne ran down the alley, her shoes silently helping her along. In a few blocks, she entered the nearby park. Thick black shadows filled the spaces beneath the heavy trees. Spots of moonlight dappled the grass and walkways like small silver coins. Before tonight, Daphne would never have walked through the park alone, and certainly never in the dark. But her new confidence chased away all fear. She wasn't afraid of the shadows.

Daphne was a shadow herself.

She spent the next few hours running through the park and the nearby streets, testing her new powers. She passed through streetlights and mailboxes and parked cars. A stray dog rushed up to her and barked. Daphne bent down and tried to pet the animal, but her hand passed through his head. The dog fled, yipping as if stung by bees.

Daphne looked up at the clock tower in the park. It was almost twelve. A chill shook her shoulders, and somehow Daphne knew that she had to get back by midnight. *Just like Cinderella,* she thought.

Daphne quickly headed home. A strong breeze blew garbage and newspapers into her path, but she walked through them all.

Back in her room, Daphne reluctantly removed the mysterious shoes, placing them gently on the floor. The digits on her bedside clock had reached twelve. A *thump* sounded. And the shoes were gone.

So there are *rules,* she thought.

The next day at school, Daphne thought of nothing but the shoes. The hours dragged by until that night, when once again she heard the thump of the shoes, bent down to grab them, and rushed outside to play in the shadows.

The next few nights, Daphne followed this routine. She put on her new shoes at

10:01. Then she drifted through her house and neighborhood as an unseen shadow, returning to her room just before midnight.

Some nights she watched people eating at restaurants, floating through the windows to listen in on their conversations. She slipped through the walls of apartments to see how other people spent their evenings. Most people were boring, she decided. They simply sat around, watching TV or their phones, or talking about their days, or doing homework.

As the nights passed, Daphne grew bolder. She traveled farther from her neighborhood, and once even drifted onto a bus. She sat next to strangers, watched passengers sleep, read books over their shoulders, and saw them pick their ears or noses when they thought no one could see them. A few times, Daphne laughed out loud. No one seemed to hear her.

On these nights when she was exploring, she had to remind herself to keep checking the time. She worried that if her shoes disappeared at midnight, she might also vanish if she were still wearing them.

I suppose I could just take them off if I needed to, she thought. *Though I'd have to walk home barefoot.*

Daphne experimented. While she stood in the shadowy park one night, she stepped out of the shoes. She gazed down. The shoes looked fuzzy, but they were still there. Everything else looked the same. The trees, the benches, the trash cans.

But Daphne felt different. She felt extremely tired, drained of all energy.

She barely had enough strength to put the shoes back on. As soon as she did, a flood of confidence surged through her body.

Daphne felt like a superhero.

It had been a week since she discovered the shadowy shoes. It was late, almost midnight. She was walking slowly through the park on her way back home.

I should probably take the shoes off, she told herself. *Just in case.*

Daphne bent down to slip off the shoes. They wouldn't budge. She sat down on a bench and pulled at the shoes. Her feet had swelled with all her walking. Now the shoes were too tight.

The girl panicked. She looked up at the clock tower. One minute to midnight.

She yanked at the shoes, but they stayed firmly on her feet.

Daphne looked around the park. She was starting to worry. Surely there was someone who'd help her. But she was alone. Then she spied a tree root sticking above the ground. An old oak at the edge of the park had roots growing above the grass. Maybe she could wedge her foot against one of them while she pulled off the shoes.

Daphne ran across the park. A dog, the same stray as before, burst down the street and began barking at her again.

Daphne turned to look.

She should have watched where she was going. Daphne's left foot hit one of the roots, and she tripped.

Her shoe slipped off as she fell. She extended her arms to catch herself. But her shadowy body was passing straight through the old tree trunk. Then both shoes fell off, grew blurry and dark, and disappeared. Daphne screamed in pain, then blacked out.

* * *

The next morning a woman who was on her way to work noticed something odd about the tree at the edge of the park. She stared, then smiled to herself and shook her head. She could have sworn that an imprint in the bark looked like a young girl's face. It was amazing what you could see in nature. She took out her phone and snapped a photo. She'd have to share it with her friends.

The woman hurried on, her shoes striking solidly against the sidewalk.

THE
WAITING
POOL

Grant was warm, but he wasn't sweating nearly as much as his father. "Ready for our new pool?" asked Mr. Costello.

Grant rolled his eyes. "Dad, it's a wading pool."

"A super-fancy wading pool," said Mr. Costello. He and Grant stood in their backyard. The sun blazed down on them from a cloudless, blue sky. The big, blue wading pool had taken Mr. Costello two hours to put together. It was twelve feet wide and surrounded by a plastic wall two feet high. A small set of plastic steps helped would-be waders climb over the edge.

"I couldn't believe it was free," said Mr. Costello. "The guy at the garage sale knocked it down to five bucks. I still wasn't sure if I should buy it. Then he comes up and whispers, 'It's yours. I don't want it anymore!' Boom."

Grant put his hand on the stiff plastic wall. "Is it OK?" he asked. "I mean, if it's OK, why did the guy get rid of it?"

Mr. Costello shrugged. "Maybe his kids got too big for it," he said. "Maybe he wanted to put in a real pool. Who knows? But you can't argue with free."

Grant snatched his hand away from the pool wall.

"What's wrong?" asked his dad.

"I don't know," said Grant, gazing at his hand. "It felt like . . ."

"It's hot from sitting out in this crazy sun. Come on, let's fill this baby up," said Mr. Costello. He walked over to the house and picked up the end of a long garden hose. Twenty minutes later, the pool was full.

"Let it warm up," said his father. "Water straight from the hose is cold."

After Mr. Costello went inside to cool off, Grant stayed out in the yard and played

Frisbee with his dog, Gump. Suddenly, Gump started barking. Grant turned and saw an old man leaning over the pool.

His stringy white hair fell past his shoulders. His skin was wrinkled like a crumpled-up piece of paper. His fingernails were long and yellow.

The man kept staring into the pool. Gump barked a few more times, and the man turned. He blinked his watery gray eyes at Grant a few times. Then a weird look came over his face. He coughed and spit and muttered words that Grant couldn't understand. He waved his arms wildly over his head and then stumbled in Grant's direction.

Grant ran toward the house, Gump running alongside and barking.

The boy reached the screen door and rushed inside. Quickly, he locked the handle. He gazed through the screen and shouted, "Go away!" But the man was gone.

He waited a few minutes to make sure the man didn't come back. Then Grant opened the door, and he and Gump stepped outside. The backyard was empty. The pool sat quietly, reflecting the blazing sun.

Grant walked over to where the ancient man had been standing. He stared into the pool. The water lapped gently back and forth against the curving plastic wall.

Grant thought something must have disturbed its surface. But there was nothing there in the clear water.

Had the hot sun made him see things? If so, why had Gump barked? The dog couldn't be seeing things, too.

* * *

Grant avoided the pool the rest of the day. But the next afternoon, two of his friends came over to check it out.

The boys splashed and played in the water, tossing a soccer ball back and forth. Even Gump jumped into the pool a few times. Eventually Grant forgot all about the strange man from the day before.

"It's pretty cool for a little kid's pool," said Grant's friend Li.

"Yeah, it's awesome," agreed his friend Rodey.

Suddenly Li got a frightened look on his face. He pointed at the center of the pool. A hand rose out of the water. Li screamed. "What's that?"

The boys stood against the curving plastic wall as the water in the middle bubbled and churned.

The hand was followed by a bony shoulder and then a head, covered in long, wet, stringy hair. It was the old man. The other boys screamed. The old man reached out to them, grasping at their legs and feet. Grant felt hard fingers trying to hold onto his right foot, but he kicked them away.

The boys climbed out of the pool as quickly as they could, tumbling onto the grass and scrambling to their feet. From a safe distance, they stood barefoot in the grass. Grant watched the old man disappear underwater.

"Get away from there, dude!" Rodey yelled to Grant.

Grant looked toward his friends, who had run toward the house. Instead of his friends, there stood two old men.

The men grew thinner before his eyes. Their backs arched and their shoulders hunched. Their hair whitened and fell out in clumps. Their arms and bare legs grew thin and frail. Wrinkles spread across their faces like spider webs. One of the men opened his mouth to speak and a tooth fell out.

"What's going on?" said Grant. "Who are you?"

The old men wore the same swimming trunks and T-shirts as Li and Rodey. They tried answering Grant, but weird sounds came from their mouths. They couldn't speak. They could only mumble.

Grant looked quickly at the pool. Where had that old man in the water gone?

Grant decided he was going to ask the old men what they had done to his friends, but his mouth wasn't working right. His tongue was thick, and his lips were numb. He raised a hand to feel his face, but the hand he saw was not his hand. It couldn't be. It was pale and flabby. The fingernails were sharp and yellow.

The back door of the house banged open. Grant's father stood there. "What are you doing in my yard?" he yelled. "Get out of here," he said, "or I'll call the police!"

"Dad! It's me," shouted Grant. But the words didn't come out that way. His voice sounded more like a growl.

"Get out, I said," shouted Mr. Costello. "Or so help me." He took a threatening step toward the men.

The two old men fled across the yard.

Grant stood there a moment longer. He saw an old dog panting at his father's feet. The dog reminded him of a dog he had owned a long time ago. What was its name again? Gumbo? Grump?

While Grant watched, the dog crumbled to the ground. Its body turned to dust and its gray hair floated off in the breeze. His father looked down at the powder that had once been their dog and cried out.

Mr. Costello covered his face with his hands. Then he stared at the old man who had not run away. "Do I know you?" he asked.

Grant tried to speak, but more of his teeth fell out.

"You look familiar," said Mr. Costello. He had a sad, confused look on his face. The man glanced around the yard. "Where's my son? What have you done with Grant?"

Grant's vision blurred. He could barely hear his father's voice. He forgot where he was. *Whose house is this?* he wondered. A single image stayed in his memory. *The water,* he thought. *I must reach the water!*

Grant turned slowly and limped toward the swimming pool. Every step seemed to last a year.

The sun burned hotter against his aging flesh. The sweat poured down his body. As the sweat dripped, it pulled pieces of his skin along with it. The bones underneath gleamed in the blazing sunlight.

Grant was only a foot away from the pool when the breeze grew stronger and the white bones crumbled to dust.

FLUSHED

The water swirled rapidly down the toilet with a loud gurgle. "Where do all the goldfish go?" asked Rachel.

"Down," said her older sister, Pamela.

The two young girls stood over the toilet in their bathroom. They had just flushed another dead goldfish — the seventh or eighth? — into the swirling waters. Its final, fishy resting place.

Rachel peered into the water. "Do you think they'll ever swim back?"

"They're dead," said Pamela. "They're gone. The water flushes them out into the ocean or something."

"What if this time the goldfish wasn't dead?" Rachel worried aloud. "Maybe it was just sleeping. Sleeping looks like dead."

"It was not sleeping. It was sick," said Pamela. She lowered the toilet lid and walked back to their bedroom. Rachel followed close behind.

Pamela flopped down on her bed and picked up a magazine. "Goldfish get sick so easy," she said, flipping the magazine pages.

"But everybody gets sick," said Rachel.

"Not me," said Pamela. "I don't even get colds."

Rachel sighed. Her throat was feeling scratchy. Her nose had been plugged up when she woke that morning too. Rachel hated colds.

"The fish wouldn't have gotten sick if you hadn't fed it too much," said Pamela, without looking up from her reading.

"But it was hungry," Rachel protested.

"How can you tell?"

"Its sad, sad eyes," said Rachel.

"Fish eyes all look the same," Pamela said.

Rachel coughed. She put her hand to her throat and rubbed it.

Pamela looked up quickly and stared at her sister.

"What?" demanded Rachel. "What's your problem?"

Pamela's eyes were wide and frightened. "Nothing. Never mind."

Rachel looked away. She did not want to get a cold. Everyone would make too much fuss.

But the next morning, she couldn't get out of bed. Her mother came into the bedroom, sat next to Rachel, and felt her forehead. "Oh dear," said her mother. "It's a fever."

"I don't have a fever," mumbled Rachel from her damp pillow.

"Shh!" whispered her mother.

The woman looked around the room, as if afraid that someone was listening to them. She looked down at her daughter and shook her head. "And you looked flushed too," she said.

"Flushed?" said Rachel quietly.

"Your face is all red, honey," said her mother. "I'll go get you a cold cloth for your forehead." She bent down close and said, "I'll tell your sister. Don't worry, Rachel. I know you'll get better soon."

Rachel watched her mother walk out of the room. *I don't have a cold,* she thought. *I don't! And Mom is right. I'll feel better soon. It's nothing.*

The next day, she felt worse. Her temperature had risen. Her throat was raw and raspy. Her cough could be heard throughout the house.

Pamela came to look in on her sister. She stood by the door with a frown on her face. "Can you please keep it down?" she said. "Everyone can hear you."

"I can't help it," said Rachel. Suddenly, she coughed again, long and loud.

Pamela looked up at the ceiling. "Too late," she said.

Outside the house, two huge gold-colored fins reached down. The fins gripped either side of the building, raised it up in the air, and then began shaking it. Screams and shouts could be heard within.

After a moment, the front door of the house, facing downward, flipped open. Rachel fell from the door and plunged through the air. She landed in a vast white bowl filled with water. As soon as she hit the surface, the water began to swirl faster and faster, and then gurgled as it disappeared into a huge, dark tunnel.

Gently, the gold fins set the house back down.

A strange voice, high above the house said, "They get sick so often."

"I know," came a second voice. "But there's nothing we can do."

The first speaker smacked its big, blobby lips. "I hate watching them go," it said. "They have such sad, sad eyes."

THE BABY
MONITOR

Samantha Moore was helping her mother organize shelves in the basement when she found it. A small blue and pink boxlike device sat on the top shelf. It had a dial; a thick, rubber antenna; and what looked like a small built-in speaker. "Is that a radio?" she asked.

Her mother glanced up and smiled. "That's your baby monitor," she said. "I haven't seen that for years."

"Does it still work?" asked Samantha.

Mrs. Moore reached up and pulled down the device. "I suppose if you put batteries in it," she said, handing it to Sam.

Sam turned a dial on the side. A crackle of static burst from the speaker. "It *does* work," she cried.

Samantha's mother began opening other boxes. "It doesn't work without the other half," she pointed out. "That's just the receiver your father and I kept in our room. The actual baby monitor went in your room, right next to your bed. That's how we could hear what was going on." Her mother tapped the device. "And that's the button we hit when we wanted to talk back to you. Sometimes you just wanted to hear my voice, then you'd go back to sleep."

Sam saw words on the back of the receiver: range: up to 100 feet. She grinned. Her best friend, Dawnay, lived less than fifty feet from her in their crowded neighborhood.

"We have to find it," said Samantha.

"That thing is so old," said her mom. Sam didn't care. Her parents had refused to get her a phone for at least another year. With the monitor, she and Dawnay could talk to each other whenever they wanted.

Samantha and her mother combed through all the boxes and the remaining shelves. They found Christmas decorations; wallpaper; a rusty, blocky machine called a typewriter; and lots of dead bugs. But no baby monitor. Sam's mother said, "I'll look through my closet later. I don't see why we would have thrown out the monitor. Especially since we kept the receiver."

By the time Samantha was ready for bed, her mother had still not found the missing half of the monitor. "Don't worry," she said. "We'll look again in the morning. I'm pretty sure it must be downstairs."

Samantha lay in her dark bedroom, dreaming of finding the monitor. She couldn't wait until she had it in her hand and ran next door to show Dawnay. Her friend would be so surprised!

"Samantha . . . ," someone said.

Sam sat up. "Mom?" she said quietly.

There was a crackle. Static. A small red light glowed on the baby monitor's receiver that sat on Sam's dresser. The voice was coming from its speaker.

"Sam . . ."

Samantha got out of bed and walked over to the receiver. She hesitated before picking up the device. She pushed the button her mother had shown her earlier. "This . . . this is Sam," she said quietly into the speaker. "Who's this?"

Another crack of static. "Sam, it's me."

"Me who?" asked Sam.

"I'm here in the house," came the crackly voice.

A cold chill prickled the back of Samantha's neck. It was hard to tell if the voice belonged to a man or a woman. Or to an adult or child, for that matter. The voice returned: "I have the other half of the baby monitor."

Well, of course. Whoever was talking must have found the rest of the device. And Sam wanted it. "Where are you?" asked Sam.

"Downstairs," came the voice. ". . . in the basement."

Sam pressed the button. "Come up and bring it with you."

There was a long pause. "It's too hard to climb the stairs, Sam."

The girl was getting colder the longer she stood barefoot by her dresser. "Just leave it on the basement steps," said Sam. "I'll get it in the morning."

The voice crackled. "Don't be afraid," it said. "You don't have to be afraid of me, Sam. I'm just a baby."

"Babies don't talk like that!" cried Sam.

"Some of us do," said the voice.

Sam stood there, not knowing what to do.

The voice returned. "Don't worry," it said. "You don't have to come down to the basement . . . I came upstairs."

Sam heard a door creak open in the hallway. Her heart thumped in her chest. She needed to reach the front door and run from the house. She ran from her room, leaving the receiver behind.

Sam saw a small shadow at the other end of the hallway. A black mass the size of a grocery bag. And it was moving.

"See? I'm right here." This time Sam heard the voice clearer than before.

The small black shape moved into the dim light cast by the nightlight in the hallway. Sam shivered as she saw a small baby, standing, holding the baby monitor in its soft, flabby arms. The baby was hairless. Its face, dark blue, was partially hidden behind the monitor. It had sharp fingernails on its tiny fingers, of which Sam counted twelve.

"Here," said the baby. "Come and take it."

"Who — who are you?" said Sam.

The baby thing took a step closer. "I'm the baby monitor," it said. "I monitor all the babies. I look after them. Just like you have a hall monitor at school. By the way, here we are in the hall. Do you have your pass, Samantha?" The baby cackled a hideous laugh. "Do you have your pass?" It rushed at the girl. Samantha heard a roar of wind and fainted onto the carpet.

* * *

The police were called the next morning. Samantha Moore's parents had found her bedroom empty, no doors or windows opened. She had disappeared overnight. It was on the news every evening for a month.

During that time, helpful friends and neighbors brought over meals and helped clean the house. A few of them finished reorganizing the basement shelves. The old baby monitor receiver was packed in a box with other items to sell or give away. It sat in a far corner of the basement.

At night, a faint crackling voice whispered from the receiver inside the box. It was muffled by the cardboard. But if someone stood close enough and put their ear next to the box they might have been able to hear. "Mom! Mom! Are you there? It's me, Samantha. I'm right here!" And sometimes, one could hear a baby laugh.

THE TALL
AND
SLENDER
MAN

"You shouldn't read those scary stories right before bed," said Charlotte's grandmother.

"I know, I know," said Charlotte, scrunched up on the sofa. She turned another page in the thick book in her lap. "Just one more," she said. "Then I'll go to bed, I promise."

Her grandmother smiled. The old woman turned to the dog at her side. "All right, Kenji. I'll let you out. Then it's off to bed for everyone."

The woman walked to the kitchen. Charlotte, who was deep in another scary story about the Tall Men, barely noticed the sound of the door opening and closing on

Kenji. The series was one of Charlotte's favorites. The Tall Men would appear in different towns and cities across the world. Whenever someone saw them, walking slowly down a street, or standing in the shadows of a building, or climbing the stairs to someone's house, they knew something bad was going to happen. The Tall Men were omens. Messengers of doom.

"Will you let Kenji back in?" asked her grandmother.

"Sure, sure." Charlotte nodded, her eyes glued to the page.

"I'm off to bed," said the old woman. She kissed her granddaughter on the forehead, and then trundled off to her bedroom at the back of the house.

Charlotte heard her grandmother call out. "Don't forget the dog!"

Charlotte put her book down and saw Kenji trotting toward the sofa. The dog was already inside. Kenji came up to her for an ear rub, but the girl stood up, ignoring him. How did the dog get back inside?

Charlotte walked into the kitchen. She saw that the back door stood wide open. But the square metal bolt of the lock was still sticking out. Still locked. Her grandmother always locked the doors, even for letting out Kenji. The older woman was afraid of thieves.

"Kenji, how did you get in?" said Charlotte quietly to herself. Kenji had followed her into the kitchen and had stopped beside her. But when Charlotte bent down to pet her, the dog was gone.

"Kenji?"

Charlotte looked behind her and watched as her dog stood up on his hind feet. A trick he had never done before. Taller and taller, the dog stretched up. His fur grew longer and became a long, thick, black coat. A coat with buttons and pockets and a collar. The slender man who was wearing the coat must have stood at least ten feet tall. He had to bend his head slightly so it wouldn't hit the ceiling.

"Where's Kenji?" Charlotte asked in a shaky voice.

"I thought I'd do your grandmother a favor," whispered the Tall Man. His skin was as white as the plaster ceiling. "You were busy with your book, and your grandmother looked so tired tonight. . . ."

The Tall Men always brought bad news. Was there something wrong with her grandmother? Charlotte ran past the man and dashed into her grandmother's room. The old woman was already in bed, pulling the blanket up over her shoulders. "Charlotte! What's wrong?" she asked.

"The man . . ." Charlotte could hardly breathe.

"What man?"

Charlotte could hear her heart beating. "The man in the kitchen."

Her grandmother was out of bed at once. She walked swiftly to the kitchen with Charlotte following.

"There's no one here," said the old woman. "You must have fallen asleep and had a dream."

Charlotte was confused, but glad that the man was gone. And that her grandmother was strong and healthy. The Tall Man certainly hadn't come for the old woman, standing there firmly in the middle of the room.

Charlotte heard a bark outside. That was her dog. Not the thing that had turned into the Tall Man. *Her* dog. Charlotte ran to the door, pulled it open, and yelled, "Kenji! Kenji!"

The dog, who always answered with a bark once the back door was open, was not in the yard.

"Kenji!"

Charlotte ran toward the street. She heard a car screeching its brakes nearby, then a dog's loud yelp. Then nothing.

She saw the shadow of a slender man standing at the end of the block. A tall, tall man.

DON'T READ THIS STORY AT MIDNIGHT!

Please. Not at midnight.

And yes, there's a reason for that. Midnight is the time I can count on you being asleep. Deep asleep. And that's important to me, because that's the only time I can slip out from underneath your bed without you seeing me.

Because if you saw me, well, the game's over.

You'd know right away I'm not human. Not with my ears at the bottom of my head and my eye — well, I don't want to get into all that.

So, if you are reading this at midnight, then please do me a favor. Do us both a favor. Put the book down. Turn out the lights. Try to sleep. At the very least, don't make any noise when you hear that slippery sound beneath you. It's just me.

Keep your eyes closed, too. If you are one of the curious types, don't say anything when you see that shadow crawling toward your door. Ignore it.

Oh, and whatever you do, do not — I repeat, *do not* — turn the lights back on.

I have a fear of sudden lights. And I can't predict my behavior when it happens. Who knows what I would do. Like pounce or something. I hate to think about it. I'm pretty sure you wouldn't like it either.

Let's keep the lights out. The dark is a much happier place for me.

And if you do happen to fall asleep, then great. It's a win-win. My friend will have time to crawl out from under the bed, too.

BIG
FURRY

"Min! Run downstairs and grab me a jar of peaches," said her mom, who was laying plates and silverware on the table for dinner.

Min bit her lower lip and didn't move.

Her mom set down the stack of plates and put a hand on the back of a chair. "Did you hear what I said?" she asked.

"Why can't Tray get them?" said Min.

"Because I asked you, young lady," her mom replied.

Min walked into the kitchen and shot a quick glance at the cellar door. Her hands began to shake a little.

Tray ran into the kitchen right behind his older sister. "Min's afraid of the dark," he chanted. "Min's afraid of the dark."

Isn't everyone afraid of the dark? thought Min.

Her mom brushed past them and hurried over to check her pots on the stove. "Now hurry up, Min," she said. "Dinner will be ready soon."

Min took a few careful steps toward the cellar door.

Her mom hurried back into the dining room. "Tray, go wash your face," she called over her shoulder. "I have to get dressed before your father gets here."

"Min's not going downstairs!" called Tray, blocking the doorway between the kitchen and dining room.

"MIN!" came her mom's voice.

Min scowled at her brother. She walked over to the cellar door and angrily yanked it open.

"See?" she said. "Does it look like I'm afraid?"

Tray said nothing. His smile vanished as he stared at the open door.

He's afraid of going downstairs too, Min told herself.

Old wooden stairs led straight down, stopped at a small landing, twisted to the right, and then slid into darkness. On the left-hand wall was a set of hooks to hang their winter coats, scarves, and hats. A small wooden box near the door held their gloves and mittens.

Min never minded opening the cellar door to grab her coat and scarf. But the thought of walking down those stairs made her shiver. Especially since it was always cold down there. Now, with winter on its way, the cold air from the cellar swirled around her bare legs as soon as she opened the door.

"Go on, Min," said her brother.

"Be quiet," she snapped. Min slowly stepped through the doorway and started down the stairs.

BANG!

Min was swallowed up in blackness. The door had slammed shut. She felt for the doorknob and turned it. It wouldn't budge. She could hear her brother giggling on the other side.

"Tray!" called Min. "Open the door!"

Tray giggled again. "I have to go wash my face," he said. Min heard his footsteps rushing away, growing softer.

"Tray!" she yelled again. Min pounded on the door. Her mom was getting dressed. Her father wasn't home yet.

Min shivered. The cold air crept up her legs. It climbed up her arms and neck.

I'm not going downstairs, Min told herself. She decided to stay where she was. She would just wait until she heard her mom return to the kitchen. *Then will Tray ever get it,* she thought, smiling.

Min rubbed her arms. The air was freezing. Her back bumped against the wall, and she felt something big and furry drop onto her shoulders. The girl jumped. She relaxed as she saw, in the dim light squeezing under the door, that it was only a coat. *Mom's winter coat,* thought Min. *Perfect.* As long as she had to wait, she decided she should at least be comfortable.

In the darkness, Min pulled the big coat tighter. The fur felt so good and warm. Along with the warmth, she felt something else. A slight vibration . . . like a beating heart. Min felt two long, hairy arms reach out from the back and wrap themselves around her.

Something growled as hot breath tickled the back of Min's neck. From below, at the bottom of the steps, came more growls. What looked like a forest of shaggy lumps with long, black tongues and furry arms, topped by tiny blazing eyes, came lumbering up the stairs.

SECTION 2

GOING SOMEWHERE?

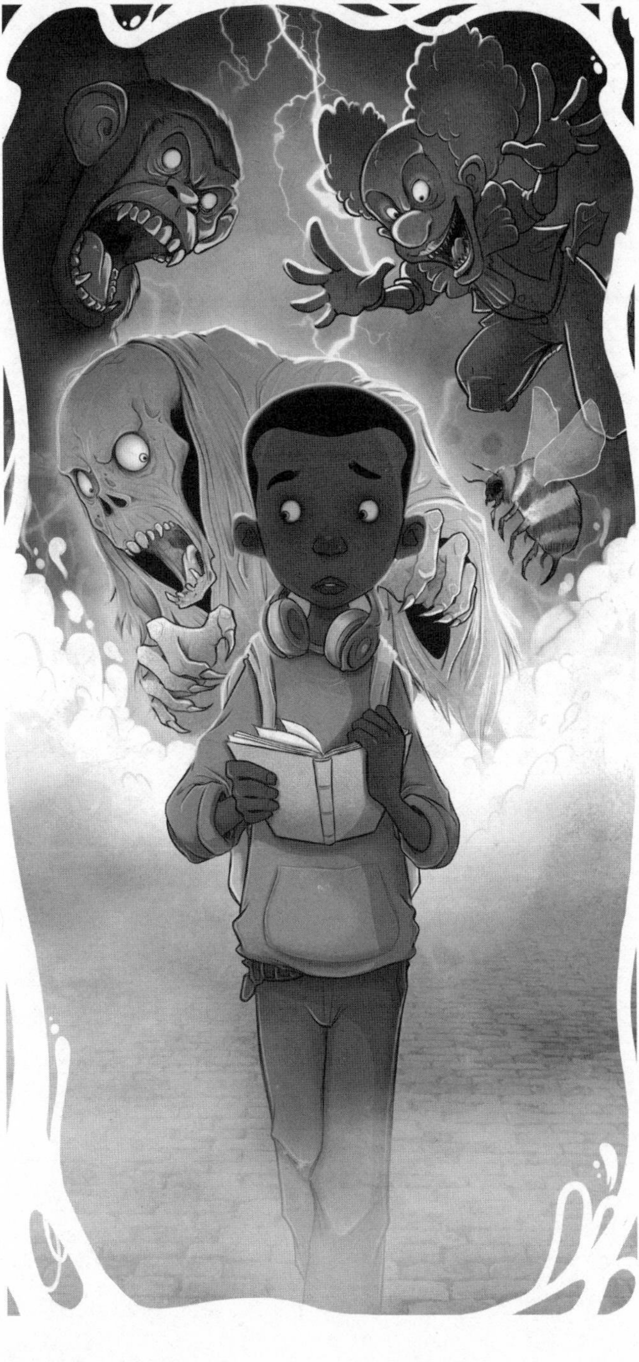

FINGERS ON THE GLASS

The wind picked up suddenly, rolling across the countryside. A storm of swiftly falling snow swallowed up cars, trucks, and buses, and their passengers.

Jada looked out the car window. It was night and the snow was falling so fast it was hard to see. She shifted into a more comfortable position in the backseat and returned to her video game.

"Bill, slow down. The road is pure ice," Jada's mother said through clenched teeth.

"It's not, and I'm barely going the speed limit," said her father. He glanced into the rearview mirror. "How you doing back there?"

"Fine," said Jada. Her head stayed down, focused on her game. It was a new version of *Boyz from Otherworld*.

She wasn't worried about the snow, but it did seem to be taking longer to get home from her cousins' than usual. There were long stretches of country road with no stoplights. Twice Jada could see cars in the ditch. Headlights angled crazily through the falling snowflakes.

One headlight caught her in the face. Jada blinked. Just before she did, she saw a weird shape on the side window. It looked like a boy's hand sliding down the wet, snowy glass. As if he was lying on the roof of the car and reaching down on Jada's side to grab the door handle.

She blinked again and the hand was gone.

What did her teacher call that? An afterimage. A shape or figure you might see after a bright glare of light. Whatever it was called, it was weird.

Jada kept playing. The car was dead quiet. The silence was broken only by a nervous gasp from her mother or a grunt from her father as he gazed through sheets of snow.

Then Jada heard another noise. It was a soft noise. It came from the window right next to her. She saw it again. A boy's hand was plastered to the outside of the glass. At least, she thought it was a boy's hand. For some reason that was the idea that popped into her head. Maybe because of her video game about boys from an alien realm. But what a silly thought: a boy lying on the roof of the car, out in the snow.

Jada blinked, but this time the hand stayed there. The fingers began to move slowly, crawling down the glass.

"Dad," Jada said softly.

"Don't bother your father," said her mom. "He's trying to concentrate."

"What is it, honey?" her dad asked.

"Bill, watch the road," said her mother.

The hand was gone.

Jada looked down at her video game. She turned it off and set it on the seat beside her. She rubbed her eyes. She was getting tired. It had been a long night visiting her cousins, with too much birthday cake and ice cream and sugar cookies. She still felt full. Her warm stomach was making her sleepy.

The noise came again. A damp, spongy thump. This time it came from the other side of the car.

The small hand was reaching down from the roof. It moved like a wet spider down her father's window. Jada gasped.

A second hand reached down to join the first. They both slid down the window. Were they going to open her dad's door?

"Mom —" she began.

"Not now, Jada," her mom said sharply, not taking her eyes off the road.

"But —"

"I said, not now."

Jada took several deep breaths. She must be dreaming. How could anyone survive on the roof of the car in this weather? Why would they be out there, even if they could survive? It made no sense.

Jada saw more headlights up ahead. Another car in the ditch? She looked out her window and immediately froze.

The boy's face was on the other side of the window, looking directly at her. His hands were braced on either side of his face. His mouth was open in a perfect O, as if he were screaming. But to Jada, all was silent, like an image on TV with the sound turned off.

After a moment, though, there was a scream. It was Jada's.

Her father, startled, turned the steering wheel. The car slid slightly on the icy road. Jada's mother yelled. Her dad braked the car and brought it to a swift, solid stop.

"What in the world?" he cried.

"Jada, what is the matter with you?" her mother demanded.

"A boy!" gasped Jada. "There's a boy out on our car. I saw him. I saw him!"

A terrified look clouded her mother's face.

"I'm not making it up," said Jada. "He's on the roof." Her voice broke. She tried hard not to cry.

Her mother glanced nervously at her husband. "Bill, what are you doing?" He had opened his door.

"There's nothing on our car," he said to Jada. "I'll show you." He stepped out into the blizzard and slammed the door shut.

They couldn't see him even a few feet from the car. Her mother panicked. "Stay right here," she ordered Jada. Then she, too, opened her door and stepped out, swallowed up in a wall of blowing snow.

Jada waited a few minutes. Were her parents out there with the mysterious boy?

Fear turned her stomach to ice. Jada rushed out of the car. "Mom! Dad!" she cried. The headlights from their car showed only a wall of snow. "Mom!" she called again.

"We're over here, honey!" called her father.

Jada pulled her cap down over her braids. She pulled her collar tight around her neck. Then she leaned into the wind and snow and trudged forward.

"Over here!" her dad called again.

Her parents were standing in the road about twenty feet from where they had stopped. A heavy oak tree, its branches weighed down with snow, had fallen across the road.

"Back to the car," said her dad. "We'll go back to Highway Three and drive around this mess."

When they reached the car, Jada's mom whispered to her. "If your dad hadn't stopped, we would have crashed right into that tree. I hate to think what would have happened."

"Talk about luck," said her dad, shaking his head.

Jada had her hand on the handle of her car door when she looked up. Some of the snow on the roof had been knocked off. The trunk of the car had a clear path through the middle of its snow cover, as if a small body had slid down from the roof and onto the ground. And there, behind the car, was a trail of footprints running away. Jada watched the footprints slowly filling up with snow, disappearing into the blizzard.

When she returned to the backseat, Jada reached down. The video game player was gone. And the seat was wet with melting snow.

THE DARKEST BRIDGE

It was midnight when the three bikes stopped in the middle of a bridge. The bridge spanned a deep ravine. Far below, a swiftly moving stream was quietly murmuring.

"What's wrong?" said Tina. "Why did you stop?"

Her older sister, Zoe, her hands still on the handlebars of her bike, looked at her and smiled. "Don't you know where we are?"

"I do," piped up a voice behind them. It was Tina's friend Nyssa. "It's the haunted bridge."

"Are you kidding me?" said Tina.

"It's true," said Nyssa. "Right, Zoe?"

The girls had gone to a scary movie in town that night. On the way home, Zoe had decided to lead them on a different route. They had ridden away from the lights of the small town toward a thick forest. After riding down a country road lined with tall trees, they reached the old wooden bridge.

"Are you telling me there are ghosts living on the bridge?" asked Tina.

Tina loved scary movies. She also loved watching TV shows about ghost hunters and listening to podcasts about weird and spooky events in history. She had never actually seen a ghost herself, but she hoped to.

"Not *on* the bridge," said Nyssa. "*Under* the bridge."

"That's not exactly the story," said Zoe.

"Tell me!" begged Tina. She had to know.

Zoe turned so she could see both girls. "It was eighty years ago tonight," she began. "Some kids were coming back from a church picnic . . ."

"A picnic at night?" asked Tina.

"It lasted all day," said Zoe. "They had a bonfire or something at night. Anyway, these kids were riding their bikes back to town. It started raining, and they were crossing this very bridge —"

Tina heard a sound somewhere on the other side of the bridge. An owl?

"The girl whose bike was the last one over the bridge hit a patch of water," continued Zoe.

"That doesn't sound good," said Tina. The owl hooted again.

Zoe said, "Her bike skidded. She plunged down hundreds of feet until she landed in the creek at the bottom!"

"Poor kid," said Nyssa.

Zoe nodded. She wheeled her bike to the edge of the bridge and looked down. The other two followed her. They all gazed into the blackness below.

"So what happened?" asked Tina. "Does she haunt the bridge? Will we see her walking around?"

"Will we hear her scream?" whispered Nyssa.

Zoe shook her head. "It's spookier than that," she said. "They say that sometimes . . . sometimes, if you're riding your bike over this bridge, it will stop and you won't be able to move."

"Why?" asked Tina.

"The dead girl needs another bike to ride home," said Zoe. "So she'll grab yours because hers is down in the water."

"That *is* spookier," agreed Nyssa.

"Wait!" cried Tina. "I can't move my bike! She's grabbed it!"

The other girls laughed.

"What's so funny?" said Tina. The fear made her angry.

"Zoe," said Nyssa, giggling. "She's holding the back of your bike!"

Zoe laughed out loud.

"Very funny," said Tina. "Let's get out of here."

"Wait!" said Nyssa. "What's that?"

They heard a faint bump. Then another.

The sounds came from behind them, toward the end of the bridge. One after another, the wooden planks creaked. It sounded as if someone was riding a bike onto the bridge.

"You're doing that!" Tina shouted at Zoe.

"No, I'm not," said her sister.

"I'm out of here," Tina said. She mounted her bike and pumped the pedals as fast as she could. Zoe was close behind her.

Nyssa shouted. "I can't move!" she said. "My wheels are locked or something. I'm not making it up. Help me!"

"I don't believe you," yelled Tina.

"Please!" begged Nyssa.

There were no lights on the bridge. Only their dim bike headlights lit the surroundings. But as Tina watched in horror, she saw a skinny white arm reach over the edge of the bridge and grab the rear tire of Nyssa's bike.

Suddenly, the three headlights flickered and went out. The girls were now in a thick darkness.

"She's got my foot!" screamed Nyssa.

Tina jumped off her bike, pushed it aside, and ran onto the darkened bridge. She felt for the nearest railing and followed it to where she had last seen her friend.

"Don't go!" shouted Zoe.

Tina walked farther and farther onto the bridge. She waved her free hand around, hoping to touch Nyssa or her bike. "Nyssa, where are you?" she called.

There was no sound except for the murmur of the stream below. Then the murmur grew louder. It became a loud hum and then a rumble.

"Nyssa!" shouted Tina desperately. "Where are you?"

The rumble grew even louder, and then a flash of light. Two lights. A huge truck was racing down the road. It roared onto the bridge.

Tina felt a small hand gripping her ankle as the lights grew brighter than the sun and smashed through the darkness. The small hand gave a sharp yank. A wave of cold air surrounded Tina as she toppled off the bridge. The truck rumbled overhead. Tina fell through the darkness. She heard Nyssa's screams from far below as she plunged down to join her.

THE
PHANTOM
TRAIN

Patricia had half a mind to stop pedaling her bike and lie down in the nearby grass. She was worn out.

"Does it ever end?" Patricia shouted to her cousin, who was riding up ahead.

"You're always so impatient," said Ross. "This road will take us right past the cow barn."

The two cousins had been biking for hours, exploring the roads and highways that skirted the boundaries of Ross's farm. Now their shadows grew longer. The sky was a deeper blue. The breeze was cool, and Patricia's legs were tired.

"It's not far now," called Ross.

The soft dirt Patricia had been riding on suddenly turned hard, gray, and flat. Ross was leading her down an old highway. Up ahead she saw two train signals, their long white arms pointing into the air.

Suddenly, the signals came alive. The orange lights flashed. Their bells rang out loud and clear as the white guard arms lowered in front of them.

Ross came to a stop and stood with his head lowered, concentrating. "There's no train coming," he said.

"How do you know?" asked Patricia, pulling up beside him.

"The ground should be rumbling," he said. "We'd feel it if a train was coming."

The bells kept clanging.

"Then why —" she began.

"Who knows?" said Ross. "Some kind of malfunction." He steered his bike to the end of the first guard arm. "Let's just go around," he said.

Patricia followed him, and they both walked their bikes to the side of the road.

"Hey!"

The kids turned and saw a car beside them. The shout came from a middle-aged man, who sat behind the steering wheel. He was sunburned and wrinkled, with a worn cap on his head. Patricia thought his car looked like it belonged in an old movie. It had fins and chrome and was painted white and turquoise.

"You kids don't want to be fooling with that train track," said the man. He didn't look at them. He stared straight ahead, gazing beyond the guard arms. "You haven't heard about the Phantom Train?" he asked.

Ross rolled his eyes.

"I haven't heard of it," said Patricia.

The man stared straight ahead. "Years back," he began, "a young man was speeding along these parts, spinning up dust for miles. Then he came down this road. Halfway Road, it's called."

"I didn't know it had a name," said Ross.

"Don't know why Halfway," said the man. "Maybe because it's halfway between here and the devil."

The man continued telling his story and kept staring straight ahead. *Maybe he's lying*, thought Patricia. Her grandma had told her that liars never look you straight in the eye.

"The kid reached this here train track," said the man. "And a train was coming. You could feel it rumble in the air. The lights were on. The rails were coming down. But the kid didn't stop. He stepped on the gas and went faster. He figured he was smart enough and his car was fast enough to beat the train. If the rails came down, so be it, he thought. He'd crash right through 'em."

Patricia couldn't wait for him to take a breath. "And did he?" she asked. "Did he crash through them?"

"Indeed he did," said the man. "Crashed through the first rail like a knife through butter and ran smack into the side of the coming train. CRACK! The car got caught somehow, stuck to the side of the train. Dragged the car and that poor kid almost a mile before the train was able to stop."

Patricia thought she was going to be sick.

"When they pulled the car off the train . . ." The man paused to swallow. "When they pulled the car off, they found the kid."

Ross's eyes grew wide. "They did?"

"Yeah, and know what they found? His body was cut right in half. From his skull down to his legs. Like two halves of an apple with the seeds showing. Like something out of a nightmare. And that's where the Phantom Train comes from.

Every so often, people who drive down this road will see the arms come down and the lights flash. And if they wait a minute, they'll feel the wind from the train."

Patricia's hair began to blow in the breeze.

"They'll feel the rumble from the tracks."

Patricia and Ross felt a vibration in their handlebars.

"That's when you know the Phantom Train is coming," said the man. "A train you don't want to mess with." He stared straight ahead through the windshield, hypnotized by the signals.

Ross turned to Patricia. "Good story," he mumbled under his breath.

"It ain't a story! I saw it!" shouted the man. "I was there!" He turned to look directly at them. The man's head was split in half. His face had only one eye, a single flaring nostril, and crooked teeth hanging in half of his mouth. The other side, the side that had been facing away from them, wasn't there.

Patricia screamed. She got on her bike and headed to the train crossing. She had to get away.

Ross pulled her back, just as the breeze became a wind, and the wind swirled into a gale. A wall of air swept over them, pushing them back from the guard arms. Light flooded the tracks. A train's horn blared across the empty fields, louder than thunder.

And as the cousins watched, a huge shadow in the shape of a train rocketed past them. It whipped at their clothes and flattened the grass that surrounded them. Patricia screamed a second time as she watched this machine from another world speeding over the tracks.

They closed their eyes against the dust and gravel swirling around them, until the wind slowly loosened its grasp. The lights were gone. The train had vanished. Ross jumped when the guard arms suddenly lifted. Finally the bells stopped.

The two cousins stared at each other.

Ross broke the long silence and turned toward the car. "Thanks, mister," he said. "You saved our lives."

But the car was no longer there. The road was empty.

NIGHT
OF THE
FALLING
STAR

"You can't come," said Eddie. "You're too young."

"I'm nine," said Ollie.

"That's too young," said Eddie. "Besides, meteors could be dangerous."

"It's not a meteor anymore," Ollie said. "When it hits the Earth, it's called a meteorite."

Their dad walked out onto the dark porch and asked why they were arguing. Eddie explained that a shooting star had landed outside town, and that all his friends were driving out to see it.

Ollie corrected him and said that a meteorite had crashed out past Paul's Valley, and that Eddie refused to take him.

"Is that what the big boom was?" their father asked.

"It crashed just an hour ago," said Ollie. "And Eddie won't take me."

Their father looked at Eddie. "Take your brother."

"He'll get in the way," said Eddie.

"Take your brother," repeated their dad. "It'll be a fun outing for you two."

Eddie groaned.

"Yes!" said Ollie, pumping his fist.

* * *

Eddie was quiet during the drive, but Ollie was too excited to sit still. "I bet we'll get there before the scientists," said Ollie. "It'll probably be too hot to touch. Of course, we might just see a big hole in the ground. The meteorite will be buried deep underground, right in the center of things. I wonder if it's magnetic. Use your phone, Eddie. See if it's magnetic when we get there. Check your compass app. See if it goes wild like it does in the movies."

"Weird," said Eddie. It was the first time he had spoken in half an hour.

"What's weird, Eddie?" asked Ollie.

His brother pulled over on the side of the road. The sun had set during their drive out. There weren't many lights this far out of town, but they could see at least twenty other vehicles parked along both sides of the highway.

"Nobody's around," said Eddie. "Pete said he was coming out."

"They're all looking at the meteorite," Ollie said.

"Somebody would be out here," said Eddie. "And it's so quiet."

Ollie had to admit that it was strangely silent. Especially if there were that many people from town together in one place.

"Well, come on," said Eddie. "Let's go take a look."

It was easy to tell which way the meteorite had landed. Clouds of thick vapor poured through the trees on the south side of the road.

At first, Eddie and Ollie had no trouble finding a path through the short grass and passing the row of trees. Grasshoppers leaped out of their way, disappearing into the dark. The farther they went, the thicker the vapor became.

"I still don't hear anything," Eddie mumbled.

"We should have brought a flashlight," said Ollie.

Ahead, in the distance, a reddish glow burned through the vapor like another setting sun. "That's it!" yelled Ollie. He was about to run toward it, but his brother gripped his shoulder.

"Listen," said Eddie.

"I don't hear anything," said Ollie.

He realized that he didn't even hear crickets. Then —

It was faint. Like a hundred people talking and shouting. It sounded as if the brothers were standing in the parking lot outside a football stadium, and the cries of the crowd barely reached their ears. The closer they got to the meteorite, thought Ollie, the louder the people from town should be.

Where were they?

Ollie and Eddie took a few more steps toward the glow. With each step, Ollie could hear the faraway cries again.

Ollie felt funny. His eyelids were heavy. His head ached. He took a few deep breaths. "I don't feel so good, Eddie," he said.

"Yeah, I'm not feeling great either," said Eddie. "Maybe it's the mist. It's hard to breathe."

"I want to go back to the truck," said Ollie.

Eddie grabbed his arm and led him in the direction of the road. Ollie could feel the warmth from the meteorite against his back as they walked. He didn't regret not getting a closer look. He felt uneasy now, and he just wanted to go home.

"Where are the trees?" asked Eddie.

They had been walking for what seemed a long time. *Are we lost? What's with all this tall grass?* Ollie wondered. They hadn't walked through any of this tall grass on the way out. The grass waved high above their heads. It was growing! "Eddie!" cried Ollie.

"Don't worry," said his older brother. "Let's just keep going. I know this is the right way."

They kept floundering through the tall grass. Soon Ollie heard the sounds of engines roaring up ahead. The highway!

"Those sound like jet planes," mumbled Eddie.

Suddenly, the jungle of grass came to an end. There was a sharp straight line of grass that marked its outer edge. Next to the grass ran a border of dirt and then a mound of hard, black tar. "This must be the road," said Eddie. He kept walking. "We must have gotten lost in that grass and ended up away from the cars."

Ollie was a few yards from the empty road when he hard a click behind him. He turned and saw a pale green snout push through the tall grass. It had eyes the size and color of basketballs. Long feelers, like the antenna on Eddie's truck, wiggled at the top of its twitching head. The creature clicked and whirred. It scooted out of the grass with sickening speed.

"Eddie, help me!" screamed Ollie. He rushed as fast as he could toward his brother. He heard the creature clicking behind him, coming closer.

When Ollie reached Eddie standing on the road, the creature stopped. The pale green head pivoted back and forth. Its long front legs twitched. With a spring, the creature flew high above them and disappeared back into the grass.

Ollie stood next to his brother on the highway. He couldn't speak. He wanted to say the word "grasshopper" but it refused to leave his dry, frightened mouth.

Now he knew why the grass was so tall. Why it appeared to be growing. Why they couldn't see the trees, and why the road looked so different from before. Everything was the same, except for them.

The grass hadn't been growing. They had been shrinking!

"It was the mist, Eddie," said Ollie. "Something in the mist."

"And that noise we heard," said Eddie. "Like people far away . . ."

With every step, they had heard distant cries. Cries of people yelling out in terror. In pain. Before they were crushed.

"Who's that?" said Eddie. "Is that Pete?"

Ollie heard the voice too. It did not come from below. This voice was loud, almost booming, and it came from up above.

He looked up and the sky disappeared. It was blotted out by the sole of an enormous shoe.

THE GIRL
IN THE
GRAVEYARD

A cold breeze blew in Bradley's face as he steered his bicycle into the old graveyard. Falling leaves, their edges sharp and dry, seemed to bite at his cheeks and his bare hands. It was almost as if the wind knew something that day. As if the air itself, the dark October air that lay huddled around the cemetery's headstones, was trying to stop the boy. It gusted against the tires and frame. It seemed as though it was warning him to take another way.

"Hey, kid! Look out!" yelled a young man who was busy raking leaves in the graveyard.

Bradley, without thinking, drove right through the pile. *Whoosh!* "Sorry," Bradley yelled back over his shoulder.

"Sorry don't cut it, kid!" the man shouted, raking more furiously than before.

Bradley grinned as he gripped the handlebars and kept his eyes straight ahead. He had never taken this shortcut home before. There were a lot of headstones to avoid and the wind was strong.

He followed the well-worn paths that led around old trees and beside rows of waving bushes. He pedaled past statues of weeping angels whose faces had been worn away by weather and time. The narrow path led Bradley near a small, spooky building that looked like an ancient temple he'd seen in his history textbook.

"Boo!"

A strange girl, her head cloaked in scarves and a cap, jumped out from behind the building and lunged at Bradley.

The startled boy swerved, almost crashing into a tree. He stopped his bike and could hear the girl giggling behind him. He turned as he shouted, "That's not funny!"

The girl was gone.

Bradley leaned his bike against the tree and quickly walked around the small temple. He thought the girl might be hiding there. When he found that he was alone, Bradley climbed back on his bike and headed down the trail.

He had only been biking for a few seconds when the girl jumped out from behind a headstone. She flapped her arms at him, then ran off. Bradley shot after her, but he quickly lost her among the rows and rows of gravestones and the growing dusk.

Angry, he turned back to the pathway.

With each minute, the sun sank lower behind the trees. More leaves drifted from the branches. The cold wind blew them toward Bradley's bike, where they swirled and then vanished behind his humming tires.

Twice more the strange girl jumped out at him, trying to scare him. Bradley kept his mouth firmly shut and tried his best to ignore her. He would merely swerve out of the way, turn his face from her, and keep pedaling.

Bradley could see the wall that marked the west side of the graveyard. Beyond that was the street that led home. It had been several minutes and the girl had not reappeared.

Maybe she's done with her stupid game, he thought. Whoever she was. Was she the little sister of the guy who was raking leaves? Bradley didn't care. His attention was on the brick wall that lay up ahead.

Although . . .

Something about the strange girl bothered him. Not the fact that she had been annoying him this whole time. It was her appearance.

She was bundled up in a swirl of scarves and a long blue coat. She wore a tight knit cap pulled down over her hair. Bradley hadn't seen her face. It had been hidden deep within the folds of her scarves, or hidden by the shadow of a nearby tree or statue. Yet the girl looked familiar.

The blue coat. The scarves. And whenever the girl ran away or waved her arms at him, she moved weirdly. Stiffly. As if it were hard for her to bend her knees and elbows. Like an action figure. Or a —

Bradley stopped his bike. In the deepening gloom, he saw the shadow of the girl moving against the dark brick wall up ahead. She was walking jerkily, like a robot. Back and forth, back and forth.

Like a doll.

Two days ago, Bradley had pulled a prank on his twin sister, Daisy. He had taken one of her dolls and would only give it back if Daisy gave him all her snacks for a month. If their mom baked cookies, for example, Bradley would be able to eat his sister's share along with his own. Daisy had reluctantly agreed in order to get her doll back.

But when Bradley returned the doll, its face was missing. He had hidden the toy behind a heater in the basement, and the doll's face had melted away, leaving only a weird, smooth mess in its place.

Bradley insisted he hadn't done it on purpose, but he was still punished. "For your carelessness," his mother had said. Bradley had been grounded for a month. Which was one of the reasons he had taken the shortcut through the graveyard — to get home quickly, before his new curfew began.

It was getting late. The girl was still walking back and forth in front of the wall. The wind was growing stronger, colder, but Bradley was sweating. He remembered how the doll was dressed. In a long blue coat and a bunch of scarves wrapped around its melted head.

The girl stopped walking. She turned and stared at Bradley.

The boy's anger returned. He wasn't going to let this bother him anymore. He wasn't going to be tricked by some bratty kid, some annoying friend of his sister's. Bradley pedaled toward the wall.

He braked a few feet from the strange girl. "Forget it," he said boldly. "I know who you are. I know why you're doing this."

It was dark within the lengthening shadow of the wall. The girl stood still. The wind tugged at the scarves hiding her face.

Bradley wondered what her expression would be. Fear? Surprise?

"You can tell Daisy it didn't work," Bradley said.

The girl stepped closer. The wind blew harder. One of the scarves came undone and fluttered down to her feet. Now Bradley could see that from the brow of her knit cap down to the scarves, she had no expression at all. The girl had no eyes, no nose, no mouth. A flat, melted smoothness was all that showed.

Bradley cried out as the girl reached her stiff robotic arms toward him and his bike. He felt the sweat pouring down his neck, his face. And then one of his eyes slid down his chin, and then his nose. And then . . . it all went blank.

STUCK

For Raj and his cousins, it was the day *after* Halloween that scared them.

Cleanup day.

All the Halloween decorations had to be taken down, wiped off, pulled apart, packed up, and hauled away. Every last glow-in-the-dark skeleton, zombie figure, and witch's cauldron. When it came to plastic pumpkins alone, there were forty-three to collect, clean, and pack away.

"So. Many. Decorations," Raj moaned.

"You didn't complain yesterday when you were collecting candy and scaring your cousins," said Uncle Dan.

Raj's aunt and uncle hosted a huge Halloween party each year at their modern home at the edge of town. Behind their house stood a much older building. The building made the perfect haunted mansion. Even before the decorations had been added, it looked like the set of a horror film. Doors hung open on broken hinges. Ceiling and wall lamps were coated with thick dust. Spider webs and cobwebs had created their own kingdom. They invaded every corner, every window ledge, and every piece of furniture.

Web duty was the worst job to have on cleanup day.

"I can't do it, Raj," whispered his cousin Christopher. "I can't do webs. Do you know how long that takes?"

"Stick with me," said Raj. "I've got a plan."

His plan was volunteering for the second-worst job. They would clean out the haunted shack. By choosing the second-worst job, they avoided the very worst, and they didn't look lazy either. It was the best Raj could come up with.

The haunted shack was a small building behind the haunted mansion. Each year Uncle Dan hid a speaker inside that played screams and bloodcurdling laughter. It was decorated with plastic pumpkin lights. A skeleton popped out of a window every few minutes.

"Everybody to their stations!" announced Uncle Dan. The cousins rushed to their various jobs.

Rumor had it that the shack was the home of bugs and rats and maybe worse. But Raj didn't mind. "At least there's not miles and miles of cobwebs," said Raj as he pulled open the squeaky door.

He spoke too soon. As soon as he and Christopher stepped inside, they walked into a wall of sticky webbing.

"Ewwwww! I told you I didn't want to deal with webs," said Christopher.

"These shouldn't be here," said Raj. "Trick-or-treaters don't even come inside the shack on Halloween."

"Uncle Dan put these here on purpose," said Christopher. "He figured we'd weasel out of web duty, like we did last year. He's trying to teach us a lesson." Christopher looked around for a stick or tool he could use to rip a path through the clingy material.

Raj fought his way inside. "Well, we're stuck with it now," he said. A thick web coiled around his legs. It was connected to the door, and as

Raj trudged forward, the door was pulled shut behind him.

Christopher had had enough of the webs. As he headed back to the closed door, the webs seemed to grow thicker. More and more of them wrapped around his legs and arms. "I can hardly move," said Christopher.

"Mmmmphhfh!" Raj couldn't answer. Webbing was tightening around his face and chest like boa constrictors.

Christopher's arms were soon bound to his sides. "This is not going to work," he said.

A high, thin sound echoed through the air. The web was trembling.

Raj saw a dark shadow moving in the corner of the shack. Eight hairy arms reached out from a thick, round body. Eight eyes gleamed.

Click . . . Click . . .

"Spider!" Raj tried to shout. But it was no use. The webbing was too thick, too strong.

A bony jaw clicked in the darkness. *Click . . . Click . . . Click.* The eight eyes focused on the struggling boys. They had made a mess of the spider's lovely web. The creature decided it was time to clean up.

Click . . . Click . . .

Crunch.

THE NIGHT
OCTOPUS

Simone stared at the wispy white curtains clawing the air, waving like silent tentacles.

Every time she visited her great-aunt Glory, she stayed in the upstairs back bedroom. It was the biggest room upstairs and had windows on two walls, making it also the brightest room. Sunlight shimmered through those curtains. Moonlight too.

Simone liked the room's old-fashioned wallpaper with its big flowers and hummingbirds. The bed was wide and comfy, covered with dozens of plump pillows. A tall blue wardrobe facing the bed had plenty of room for her week's worth of clothes.

"What do you think, Fred?" Simone asked as she dropped an orange ball of fur onto the bedroom floor. Her new kitten bounced onto the bed. He pawed a few times at the soft pink blanket and started to purr.

"Glad you like it," said Simone.

Aunt Glory insisted that all the windows in the house stay open in the summer. If Simone closed them before she went to bed, she would find them open again in the morning. The old woman made sure the windows were open as she made her nightly rounds. "Fresh air is good for the soul," she would say.

Tonight, Simone wasn't thinking of her soul when she stared at the open windows. Simone didn't like what the breeze did to the curtains.

They moved.

The curtains fluttered without a sound in the light breeze, grasping at the air. The waving fabric reminded her of the arms of an octopus.

During a school field trip to the aquarium, Simone and her friends had walked through a dark tunnel enclosed by glass. Sea creatures of all sizes and colors drifted above and beside them. Simone was startled by a large octopus, its long, rubbery arms reaching toward her. The suckers stuck to the glass, reminding

Simone of dozens of ugly little mouths. The octopus's eyes, large as softballs, seemed to stare at her. Its body ballooned with air. Its sticky mouths opened and shut.

Frightened, Simone ran down the dark tunnel as the octopus followed her. Its tentacles twisted ever so softly in the deep, dark water.

Up and down the fabric moved. Curling and uncurling. In short, the curtains freaked Simone out.

There was nothing she could do about it except lie back down on the mountain of pillows and try to sleep.

Later that night, Simone woke up with a start. She sat up in bed. She had dreamed that something soft was touching her face.

Simone stared at the wispy white curtains.

Moonlight was sifting through the window. Just like every other night, the curtains were performing their weird, watery dance in the breeze. Curling up and down, they reached into the room.

A *snow-colored octopus*, thought Simone. White tentacles drifting through a dark, giant pool. A pool filled with drowned flowers and hummingbirds. Now and then the breeze would shift, and the tentacles seemed to reach for the bed.

Fred meowed.

"It's all right," said Simone, petting the kitten. "Go back to sleep." By comforting the kitten, Simone felt a rush of courage. Fred meowed again as the sound whispered through the room, but the girl was soon asleep.

In the morning, Simone woke up full of energy. The room was brilliant with sunlight and the curtains were still. She could smell the delicious aroma of homemade breakfast. Simone pulled on her robe and quickly joined her great-aunt in the kitchen.

"Hope you slept well, honey," said Aunt Glory, pouring a glass of orange juice for her great-niece.

"Yes, thanks," mumbled Simone. "It was just a little cool with the windows open."

"Well, that's funny," said Aunt Glory with a frown. "Because last night I thought I'd try it your way."

"What do you mean?" Simone asked.

The old woman stirred a pot on the stove. "I heard on the TV last night that it might get cold," she said. "So I went in while you were asleep and shut the windows. They were closed all night long."

Her great-aunt added: "By the way, where's that precious little kitten of yours?"

Simone froze. She hadn't seen Fred all morning. He should have followed her into the kitchen. The girl ran back to her bedroom. She didn't see Fred sleeping there, as she had hoped. When she had woken up, she threw aside the covers to hop out. Fred couldn't still be trapped under there, could he?

Simone straightened the sheets, but Fred was not there. Instead, Simone saw claw marks, ripping the blanket. The marks made straight, even lines running toward the window. It was as if the kitten had been pulled in that direction. Pulled by something that was able to reach inside the room with a long, long arm.

THE
HORNLOCK

Larry was running down the alley a dozen blocks away from his house. Except for the frightened boy, the alley was empty.

Whap . . . whap . . .

The pounding of his shoes echoed off the walls of the garages lining his path.

Darkness closed in on him. Larry locked his eyes on the streetlight at the end of the alley. If only he could reach the light before . . .

Before it caught him.

Before it ripped him to shreds with its four massive claws.

He had to reach the light. But the faster Larry ran, the faster the streetlight seemed to move away from him.

Larry halted to catch his breath, leaning against a garage for support. Goosebumps prickled the back of his neck. The moaning. He could still hear the strange, high-pitched moaning behind him.

It was not the wind that howled. It was the thing. The beast.

The Hornlock.

The creature was a family curse. For years it had hunted them. It began decades earlier when his grandfather had been killed in a strange hunting accident. It was no bear that had attacked him. It was something much worse.

And now the same creature had found Larry.

Larry pushed away from the garage and dashed toward the streetlight. This time the light stood still. It didn't glide farther away like before. The lamp's glow grew brighter and brighter.

The howls grew louder. Closer.

Strength was draining from Larry's body. His lungs burned. His chest tightened with a knot of pain. He couldn't feel his feet. Larry had been running for so long, he didn't know what time it was. He only knew that it was late. And dark. He couldn't even remember what day it was.

Another howl ripped through the night. Larry lowered his head, gritted his teeth, and strained with all his muscles. He had to reach the end of the alley.

Bang!

The light went out. The boy looked up. The streetlight was blocked by a large shadow. The shadow howled and reached out with four powerful arms. Deadly talons at the ends of the paws shined green with an eerie light.

The boy's shoulders were gripped tightly.

Larry screamed.

"Larry! Larry!" came a voice.

Larry opened his eyes and saw his mother. His bedroom was gone. Then he remembered he had decided to sleep out on the front porch that night. It was a cool summer night, and the sound of crickets had lulled him to sleep. His mother was sitting on the edge of the air mattress he slept on, shaking him awake.

It was just a dream, he thought. A stupid dream about a monster, because he'd been reading horror comics before bed.

"What time is it?" he said.

"It doesn't matter," said his mother. "Now hurry up and get out of bed. We don't have much time."

"What's going on? Where's Dad?"

A man's scream shook the house. Larry threw the covers off and hopped up from the bed. A dozen comics spilled off the sheets. He was wide awake now.

"Larry, don't!" cried his mother. The boy shrugged his mother's hand off his shoulder and ran into the house.

The house was dark, but he could still see from the light of the streetlamps outside filtering through the windows. He turned a corner, heading into the living room. A face jumped into view. His father. He looked shocked. No, he looked terrified!

"The Hornlock, Larry!" said his father. "The Hornlock is in the house!"

And this time, it was not a dream.

SECTION 3

WATCH OUT!

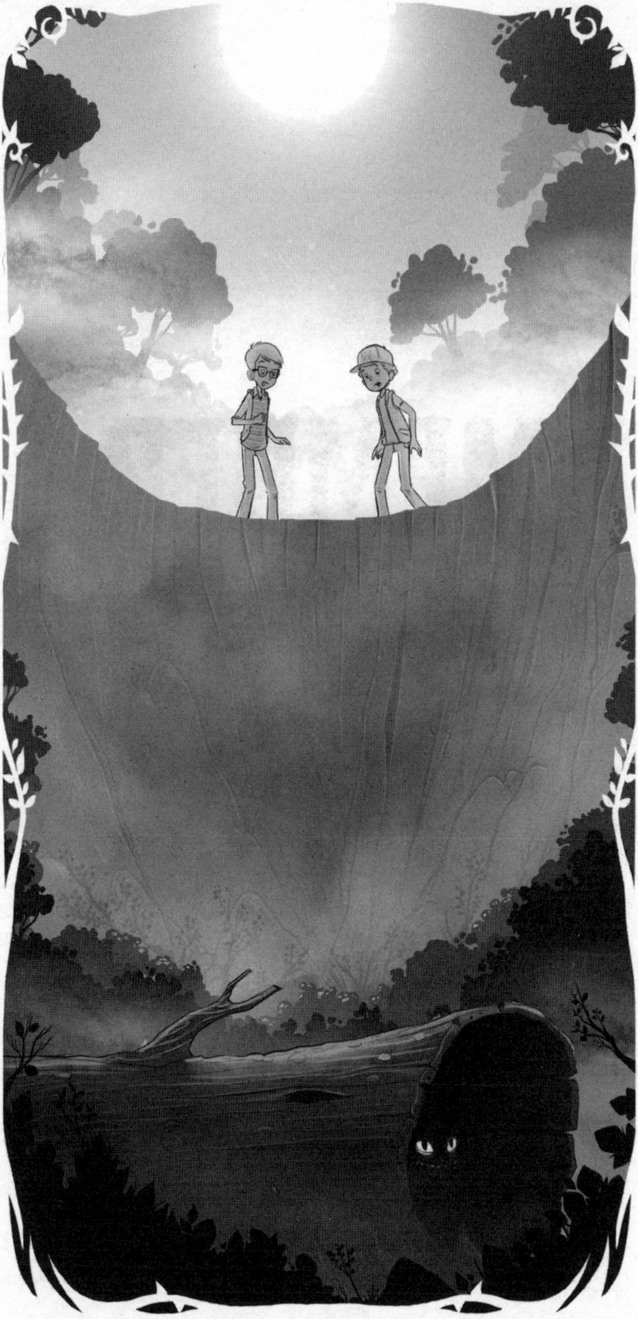

MEMBER OF THE BAND

The orange door opened with a rusty squeal, like an animal in pain.

"Sounds like B sharp," joked Cameron.

"Sounds more like someone dying," said Jesse.

The two boys, carrying their black clarinet cases, entered the old Serling Middle School building. The halls were empty. Dust and old papers littered the floors between rows of lockers on either side, the narrow doors firmly shut.

"Hello!" said Cam.

Hello, hello, hello, returned the echo from the empty hallways and hollow classrooms.

"This place is spooky. Anyway, I think the band room is that way." Cam pointed.

The boys walked toward the end of the long hall. "That echo was creepy," whispered Jesse. "It didn't sound like your voice."

"Sure it did," said Cam. "It's an echo." He burst out with another "Hello!"

Hello, hello, hello . . .

A fire had damaged the boys' regular school, so classes and sports practices were shifted to several other schools in the district. After weeks without rehearsals, the music director, Mr. Garfield, finally found the band a new home. They were using the old rehearsal room in the empty Serling building.

Cam and Jesse could see light slanting out of a doorway up ahead. They heard chairs and music stands scraping against tile floor. Mr. Garfield and some students were probably setting up the room for practice.

"Hey, what's that?" said Jesse. He began walking down a dim hall that led away from the band room. Cam followed.

"Check it out!" said Jesse. "It's an old mural."

The mural took up an entire wall. It showed students with their musical instruments. The entire mural was fading. Above the crowd of musicians floated a banner that read: FOLLOW THE BAND.

"Ha," Jesse said with a snort. "Guess what Mr. Garfield is going to say?" He pointed to the faded figure of a boy carrying a saxophone.

"We need a saxophone," Cam replied. "That's what he always says. Every rehearsal. 'Doesn't anyone want to learn the saxophone?'"

The boys heard more band members arriving, so they walked back to the rehearsal room. As they stepped away from the glass cabinets and the old mural, Cam thought he heard a soft sound behind him. The sad wail of a saxophone far, far away.

But during rehearsal, Cam forgot about the mural. He was caught up in the challenge of making his clarinet blend together with all the other instruments in the band. At different points in the song, different musicians or sections would carry the melody.

Mr. Garfield was always fun. He energetically led them through piece after piece, until he put his baton down for the last time. Cam couldn't believe that two hours had passed.

"Great work, clarinets," said Mr. Garfield to the five clarinet players. "Lovely sound. I just wish . . . Doesn't anyone want to learn the saxophone?"

Cam and Jesse looked at each other and laughed.

As the director shouted out times and dates for the next rehearsals, the students were busy putting away their instruments, snapping cases shut, shuffling sheets of music, or hoisting huge bags over their shoulders.

Cam whispered to Jesse, "I've gotta make a pit stop. Wait here for me."

Jesse nodded.

Cam wandered for several minutes before finding the restrooms. As soon as he had finished and stepped out from the bathroom, he sensed something was different. The hallways seemed darker. All the lockers were open. Their narrow metal doors had swung loose. They were full of shadows. Cam was certain they had been closed before he'd used the restroom.

He sprinted to the band room. The lights had been turned off and everyone was gone. "What's going on?" he said to the empty room. Only his clarinet case, still sitting on his chair, remained. The boy rushed to the doorway and yelled, "Jess!"

Jess, Jess, Jess . . .

Silence, and then —

"Down here. By the mural."

"I told you to wait for me," said Cam, rushing down the hallway. Wait. Where was Jesse? The hall was empty.

He called his friend's name again. No answer this time. He walked farther down the hall. Shadows hovered like a fog. The exit sign at the far end of the hall was smashed and dark. Cam tried opening the door, but it was stuck. He backed up and shouldered it hard. It didn't budge. He'd have to exit the way he came in, through the squeaky orange door.

Cameron did not especially like the dark. He gripped his clarinet case firmly and began to run.

Once past the cabinets, he told himself, *turn to the right, and you'll see the orange door.* But as he approached the mural, he saw dozens of hands and arms reaching out from the wall. It was too late to stop. He tried to swerve, but the arms were long. A crowd of hands swarmed around his body, pulling at his clothes, his hair, his instrument case. Fingers wiggled and clawed.

Just as suddenly, it all stopped. Cam felt cold. Darkness closed in around him. He wanted to yell for Jesse again, but when he opened his mouth, nothing came out.

A small light caught his attention. It seemed to be a tiny window. No, as he walked closer, he realized it was a pair of eyeholes in the wall. Level with his own. Cam cautiously put his face to the holes and gazed out.

He was staring into the very hall where he had stood a moment before. It was no longer empty. A boy wearing faded blue jeans, a faded green sweater, and faded brown shoes was staring at Cam. In his hand he carried a faded black instrument case. Cam recognized the case. It was for a saxophone.

The kid looked so happy, happier than anyone Cam had ever seen before. The boy smiled. "I've waited so long for my turn," he said. "But don't worry." He turned toward Cam. "I'll be back. You'll all get your chance."

Cam couldn't move. He was frozen in place. The boy with the saxophone walked down the hallway and out of sight. Cam was part of a new band now.

THE
HUNGRY
SNOWMAN

THE
HUNGRY
SNOWMAN

Arden pushed open the metal gate to the backyard, sending half a dozen small icicles cascading off the bars and shattering on the cold sidewalk below. He hitched his backpack up on one shoulder, closed the gate behind him, and trudged farther into the deep snow in the yard.

His sister, Rosie, was there, wrapped up in scarves and mittens and a cap. She was doing something to the snowman he had built the day before.

"What are you doing?" asked Arden.

"I'm feeding him. He's hungry," said Rosie.

"He's not a living thing," said Arden. He had just been learning about biology during his science unit that day at school. He had memorized the three things that defined life. "It doesn't move, it doesn't breathe, and it doesn't eat. It's not alive."

Rosie was patting the snowman's mouth. "Poor snowman hasn't eaten all day."

"What's that stuff on his face?" asked Arden. He peered closely at the snowman. "Is that birdseed?"

"I got it from the feeder," said Rosie.

"He looks like he's got freckles," said Arden. "Or measles."

"If the birds come to eat the birdseed," said Rosie. "Maybe the snowman will eat the birds."

"Gross!" said Arden.

"We eat birds," Rosie explained calmly. "Mom says we eat turkeys and chickens."

"Not me," said Arden. "From now on, I'm a vegetarian."

"What about chocolate peanut-butter cups?" the little girl asked. She knew those were her brother's favorite snack.

"Candy isn't meat," said Arden.

Rosie kept patting birdseed onto the snowman's face and humming. Arden was disgusted. He tromped out of the backyard and into the house.

* * *

The next morning, on his way to the back gate, Arden stopped to glance at the snowman. He almost dropped his backpack. He couldn't believe it. There were bird feathers stuck to the snowman's face. One actually poked out of the twigs and stones that made up the snowman's mouth.

Maybe the seed actually attracted some birds to the snowman, he thought. Arden suddenly felt as if he was going to lose his breakfast. Then the sick feeling turned into a small ball of anger. Why did Rosie do this? Why did she keep ruining his snowman? Arden lashed out and kicked it. He shoved at the large balls that made up the figure's middle and head until they lay on the ground in a messy, snowy heap.

Arden turned. He saw Rosie watching him through the window. Arden just shook his head at her and headed toward the gate.

* * *

That afternoon, when Arden returned home and stepped through the backyard gate, his anger returned. The snowman had been put back together. *Rosie must have been out here again,* he thought. Arden sighed, letting a puff of breath into the freezing air.

Arden trudged up to the snowman. Something was different. As the boy looked closer at the snowman's face, he grew angrier. Rosie had removed all the birdseed, but she had replaced it with something else. Chocolate peanut-butter cups ringed the snowman's mouth. *Arden's* peanut-butter cups! Ten of them. This was going too far.

Arden pulled off a glove and reached toward the chocolate treats stuck on the snowman's face. They were not going to stay out here, wasted in the cold. His attention was on the candy, but he should have looked more closely. He should have noticed the small drop of saliva that oozed out of the snowman's mouth. As the boy's bare fingers touched the first chocolate cup, it was too late.

The teeth felt like ice against his skin.

Rosie was inside the house, watching from a window. "The poor snowman *was* hungry," she said. As she closed the curtains and turned away from the window, the little girl frowned.

THE
BALLOON

It looked like an ordinary balloon to Vance Green as it flew over his neighborhood.

Except for one thing . . .

Instead of drifting with the wind, the balloon was locked in an orbit. It seemed to be traveling in a circle above the houses and trees along Oak Street and Madison Lane.

The balloon was silent, but Vance and his friends made plenty of noise as they phoned and texted each other about it.

"Over my house again," Vance shouted into his phone to his friend Rufus. He texted the same information to his other three friends, who were all watching the strange balloon from their various yards.

"Same here!" shouted his friend Rufus.

"Heading this way again," texted Tonio.

"Vance," said his father, who was hosing off the patio furniture in their backyard. "Can you keep it down? You and your friends are always so loud!"

"Gotta go, Rufus," Vance said into his phone before hanging up. "It's that balloon, Dad." He jumped up and down and pointed to the sky. "It's coming back. It keeps coming back!"

"Fine, it's a balloon," said his father, staring up and shielding his eyes with his hand. "Do you have to be so noisy about it? This used to be such a nice, quiet neighborhood —"

"'Before you cute little kids got older.' Yeah, yeah, I know," interrupted Vance. His father reminded him of that at least once a day.

"I'm going inside," said his dad, setting down the last patio chair. "I'm going to watch my cop show. At least that will be nice and quiet."

Vance felt his phone buzz in his pocket and pulled it out. "6TH TIME," texted Rufus.

"I thought it was 7," sent Irene.

While the sun set, Vance stood in his yard and kept watch. Again and again Vance saw the object float over the weathervane on the Greens' rooftop and then disappear past the elm trees next door. It followed the same orbit above the same few houses: Vance, Irene, Tonio, Gabe, Rufus, Vance.

Then something changed.

"It's lower," texted Tonio from across the street.

"RUNNING OUT OF AIR???" texted Gabe.

"IT'S BIG!!!!" shouted Rufus from next door.

"Rufus! Keep it down," said his mother.

Vance waited for the balloon to sail into view from Rufus's house next door. His friends were right. The balloon seemed larger and was definitely lower to the ground. The blue-violet sphere winked in the fading sunlight. It barely cleared the highest branches of the elm tree in Vance's yard.

When Vance saw it earlier, he thought the balloon was a standard size, maybe eight inches across. Now that it was floating closer, Vance guessed it was more like a few feet across — possibly bigger.

"REALLY BIG!" texted Irene. "Maybe ten feet across."

Huh? It isn't that big, thought Vance. It had floated out of sight just seconds ago.

"Tonio," sent Vance. "How big do u think?"

Tonio didn't reply right away like he usually did. A few minutes later, this message came: "Lower now. It's in my yard!"

"I'm coming over," sent Rufus.

Vance, too, stuffed his phone into his pocket and headed across the quiet street. He saw Irene and Rufus running along either side of him. When they reached Tonio's backyard, Gabe was already there.

"Where'd he go?" asked Rufus.

Gabe frowned. "I came right over," he said. "No one was here."

The four friends glanced quickly around the darkening lawn. They started yelling for Tonio, but Tonio's dad yelled out the window telling them to be quiet.

"He just texted all of us," said Irene. "Where did he go?"

"And where's that crazy balloon?" asked Vance.

The yard was empty. Four heads tilted upward, four pairs of eyes scanned the violet sky.

"There!" shouted Rufus. "It's back over my house again."

Hooting and hollering, each of them ran back to their own yard to track the weird object.

Vance stood behind his house again, stared up, and waited. And waited.

"Rufus, where is it?" he texted.

Rufus didn't answer. Vance ran to the fence that separated their two yards and peered over. Rufus was gone.

"I SEE IT!" came a message from Irene. "Rolling on the grass."

Vance turned quickly and ran to the other side of his yard. He pushed past the bushes and stepped into Irene's yard. He wanted to catch a close-up of the growing sphere.

Irene wasn't there. He called out for her a few times, but there was no answer. Instead, Irene's older sister Debbie stepped outside and looked at him. "What are you yelling about?" she demanded.

"Where's Irene?" Vance asked. He had a sick, cold feeling in the bottom of his stomach.

"How should I know?" said Debbie. She rolled her eyes and walked back into the house.

Vance's phone buzzed. He looked down and saw a smiley face with its tongue sticking out. Gabe!

"Gabe, u there?" texted Vance.

Gabe sent back: "Cool. It's rolling over the yard. Wonder where it's going."

A full minute went by.

Vance stopped texting and called Gabe on the phone. It rang a few times and then went to voicemail.

What's happening? thought Vance. He slowly left Irene's place and walked past the bushes into his own backyard. His dad was standing there.

"Dad! Dad! That balloon —" Vance started.

His father interrupted him. "I was wondering where you went, buddy," he said. "I was afraid you were going to miss it."

Vance frowned. "Miss what?" he said.

His father smiled. "The balloon we ordered."

"Ordered?" said the boy.

"Well, I certainly couldn't afford it on my own," said his father. "All the parents chipped in. It's the best we could do."

Vance felt a cold breeze at his back. He turned slowly and saw the balloon rolling

across the lawn toward them. It was huge —
a dark sphere, almost as large as a hot-air
balloon.

His dad nodded. "Maybe now we can have
some peace and quiet around here. Just like
it used to be. Make the neighborhood a great
place again."

The balloon rolled closer and closer without
making a sound. All Vance could see was a
wide, stretching blue-violet wall. It grew
and grew . . .

"Dad!" shouted Vance.

The balloon rolled over the boy, and
suddenly he was gone.

Vance's father stood in the backyard alone.
The man noticed something shining in the
wet grass. He reached down and picked up
Vance's phone. Then he took a deep breath.
He listened to the faint chirp of crickets and a
bird singing softly in a nearby tree.

"So peaceful again," he said.

Then he walked quietly back into his house.
The balloon rose straight up into the night
sky. It was silent, except for a few faint sounds
from within the sphere. Sounds that someone
might mistake for the noisy screams of
children.

A HAND IN THE DARK

Jasmine raced down the blue, glowing hallway, her ticket stub in one hand and a bucket of popcorn in the other. The ticket-taker, a teenage boy with a smirk, had told Jasmine "her boyfriend" was waiting for her.

Boyfriend? Angus was just a good friend. A partner in crime. It had been Angus's idea to go see the silly monster movie instead of working on their world history project that Saturday morning.

As she ran down the dim corridor, she passed a poster for the movie they were planning to see — *Absorbo*. A blobby monster made of goo that could change shape and eat people. Talk about stupid!

Jasmine spotted Angus leaning against the wall outside the theater. He was chewing on a licorice stick. "Sorry I'm late," said Jasmine.

Angus shrugged as if to say, "No big deal." He gestured toward the door and they both made their way into the dark theater.

No one else was there. *Perfect,* thought Jasmine. It would be cool to have an entire movie theater to themselves.

After several previews, the movie finally started.

"Where did you hear about this movie?" asked Jasmine.

"Online somewhere," Angus mumbled. "Should be fun."

"I promise I won't scream at the scary parts," Jasmine said.

"Me too," Angus said with a grin.

Jasmine thought of that promise after only ten minutes. The monster looked horrible. It was a mass of some weird jelly-like substance made by a mad scientist. And after it killed the scientist, it took his shape. Then it started attacking people who worked with him. It killed its victims by absorbing their bodies into its gooey body.

Gross!

When the monster lunged toward its next victim, Jasmine let out a scream. She hadn't meant to. Angus only grunted. But what was worse, she'd grabbed onto Angus's hand. Totally embarrassing.

But Angus hadn't let go. Hmm . . . was he her boyfriend after all?

"I'm glad you picked this movie," said Jasmine.

"The monster is so stupid, right?" he said.

Jasmine giggled. "Like they see the monster on the other side of the room and they still don't run away," she said. "They just stand there."

Another boy walked into the theater, holding a bucket of popcorn. *So we won't have the theater all to ourselves,* thought Jasmine. *Oh well.*

"Oh, you already have popcorn," said the new boy.

Jasmine looked at him, standing in the shadows. Was he talking to them? How rude. As he stepped toward the light from the screen, Jasmine could see his face. It was Angus.

"Jasmine," said the new arrival, "I'm sorry I'm so late, but —" The boy froze. He wasn't looking at Jasmine. He was looking past her. His face grew pale, and he dropped his bucket of popcorn, kernels falling all over his jeans and shoes.

"What?" asked Jasmine. Angus was still holding her hand. But his hand had suddenly turned cold and wet.

She was afraid to turn and look at Angus, the one sitting next to her. She was afraid of what she might see.

"Jasmine!" screamed the standing boy.

The girl felt the hand she was holding onto grow wider, fatter, gooier. It slid up her arm and began absorbing her into its dark, jelly-like mass.

THE
WIZARD
OF
AHHHHHHS!

Jonica screamed in terror.

But it was a bad scream, and it wasn't at the right time.

"No, no," said Mrs. Cartright, jumping up from her seat in the audience. "You scream *after* the flying monkeys land, not before. Wait till their paws hit the ground."

Jonica had always dreamed of playing Dorothy in *The Wizard of Oz*. But now that she had the role in her school play, she wasn't so sure she really wanted it. Dorothy was in every scene. She had a lot of lines to remember. And she had to remember when to stand, when to sit, when to speak. When you pick up Toto, hold him at your side, not in front of you.

Always have your face half turned toward the audience so they can hear you. It was a lot harder than she'd imagined. As if that weren't enough, the ruby slippers were too tight.

They did the scene again, and Jonica got the timing of the scream right. It still wasn't a good scream. She was feeling tired. The whole cast was tired. And to top it off, the rope that held one of the flying monkeys had broken, and the monkey had landed on top of the Cowardly Lion.

"All right, everyone," said Mrs. Cartright. "I think that's good for tonight. Terrific work. Alex, your makeup needs a little work. You look like a zombie, not the Tin Man. We'll have to work on that. OK, cast. Tomorrow right after school, we get to work again."

Jonica joined the other girls in their dressing room. She thought about changing out of her costume and wig, taking off the uncomfortable slippers, and putting on her regular clothes. But she was so tired.

Jonica plopped down in the big armchair against the wall. She thought, *I'm just going to close my eyes for a little while.*

She said goodbye to the other girls as they left, but she didn't open her eyes.

When she did open them a while later, she jumped up. She looked at the clock over the door. She had slept for more than an hour! Her parents would be worried.

Crash!

It sounded like something had fallen onto the stage. Jonica rushed out of the dressing room, still wearing her costume. Had the set fallen over? Did part of the roof cave in?

Jonica wound her way through the props and the scenery — all of which looked normal — and reached the front of the stage. Nothing was out of place. Nothing had fallen. The stage was empty and quiet, like the rest of the auditorium. In fact, Jonica was the only person there.

She shivered. Although Jonica loved being onstage and getting all the attention and applause during a show, an empty theater was creepy.

She headed back to the dressing room. Her house was a few streets away. It wouldn't take her long to reach home once she had changed out of her costume.

Jonica wound her way back through the scenery. She passed cardboard trees and Styrofoam crows. The flying monkeys were hanging from wires overhead. The castle of the Wicked Witch was merely a painting on a big flat of canvas.

Where was the dressing room? It was taking her a lot longer to go back than it had to run onto the stage. Jonica hadn't realized there were so many props. So many trees. The scenery was actually quite good. There were some truly talented kids in set design, she decided.

The painted scenes of thick forest and distant mountains looked beautiful. Realistic. They looked so real she imagined the branches waving in the wind and clouds drifting past the mountains. Were those birds twittering among the trees?

She saw the scenery was clearing up ahead. *Finally,* Jonica thought. But a few steps later, she walked out from the shadow of the trees and into a forest clearing. Grass cushioned her feet. Stars twinkled in a deep blue sky. The tree branches *were* waving in a gentle warm breeze.

Where am I? she thought.

She was not outside the school. She hadn't walked through a doorway. If she were outside the school, she would've seen lights from the houses in her neighborhood. But the only light was starlight, and the glow of a moon somewhere behind the trees.

"Oh!" Jonica stepped on something soft. She bent down and saw a small, dark shape. She put out her hand and felt fluffy ears. It was Toto, the prop dog she used as Dorothy's faithful pet. Stuffing was falling out of the fake fur.

Who would rip it apart like this? Jonica wondered. She remembered how her real dog, Stella, had chewed up one of her favorite stuffed animals. This was worse.

Something gleamed beyond the trees on the other side of the clearing. Out stepped the Tin Man carrying his ax.

"Alex," she said. "Alex, is that you?"

This Tin Man was much taller than Alex, who played the part. And it wasn't Alex's costume. This tin head looked more like an iron helmet. Starlight shone on sharp edges and spikes sprouting all over its body. This Tin Man's nose was a long drill. Its red eyes glowed like distant traffic lights.

"Where's Alex?" Jonica shouted.

The Tin Man came closer. Jonica saw something red on the edge of the huge ax. What was going on? Where was she?

The Tin Man raised his weapon.

"Don't!" shouted Jonica.

Just as suddenly, the figure dropped the ax. Slowly he backed away from Jonica, step by step, until he was lost in the shadows of the trees.

"What was that all about?" she said aloud.

A deep growl rumbled behind her and rippled through her body. Jonica turned to see a massive lion stalking toward her. A real lion. It flattened itself against the grass. The real grass. The mighty creature balanced on its great paws. Black claws gleamed in the starlight. It was getting ready to pounce.

Jonica remembered the ax lying in the grass directly behind her. If she was careful . . . if she could just reach back and . . .

Jonica screamed in terror.

This time it was a good scream. And her last.

LITTLE IMPS

"Isabel, hurry up! I need to use the bathroom!" Hattie pounded on the door as she shouted to her sister inside. "Pleeeeeeeeease!"

Her older sister, Isabel, did not answer.

"I can hear you in there," called Hattie. "Just let me in for a second."

Still no answer.

"You are just rude!" said Hattie. "You're an imp." She felt powerful saying the word her elderly neighbor, Mr. Slater, had used when describing some noisy neighborhood children. "A big, fat imp!"

"Who are you calling an imp, imp?" asked Isabel. The older girl appeared at the other end of the hallway, still in her pajamas and rubbing her eyes as she stepped out of her bedroom. Hattie's jaw dropped open.

"But Isabel," said Hattie, "you're in the bathroom."

Isabel yawned. "Really? Then why am I standing over here?" she asked.

Hattie turned back to the bathroom door, confused.

Isabel walked down the hall and stopped at Hattie's side. "You're obviously wrong," she said. "I'm right here. Mom must be in there." Isabel pounded on the door. "Mom, let us in."

A familiar voice called from the kitchen at the other end of the house. "You two need to get ready for school. It's getting late. And stop with all the yelling!" she yelled.

The sisters stared at each other. Who was in the bathroom if it wasn't their mom? Isabel grabbed the door handle.

"It's locked," Hattie pointed out.

Isabel rattled the handle. "No, it's just stuck."

The older girl made a fierce turn of the handle, then shoved the door open.

Once inside, the two girls froze. Wet towels covered the floor. One was draped over — and into — the toilet. Water was running in the sink. Toothpaste had been squeezed onto the walls. Baby powder was sprinkled on the floor and over the counter.

"Who made this mess?" asked Isabel.

"I thought it was you," said Hattie.

"Not me," she said. Isabel pointed to the mirror.

Hattie stood next to her sister and peered into the mirror over the sink. They could see the rest of the room reflected in its shiny surface. But there was something else. The closet door was moving.

Hattie turned around quickly. The real closet door, the one between them and the bathtub, was shut, like it normally was. In the mirror, however, the door was slowly opening.

As Hattie stared into the mirror, she saw a small creature, with pink, scaly skin and yellow cat's eyes, peek around the closet door. Baby powder covered the creature's skin. Toothpaste was smeared over its dark red lips. The creature widened its toothy smile and then stuck out its tongue at Hattie.

"How rude!" said Hattie. "Did you see that?" she asked her sister.

But Isabel was gone. A flash of pink caught Hattie's eye. She glanced back at the mirror and saw her sister being pulled into the mirror's closet by the little scaly creature. When she looked back at the real closet behind her, it was normal. Hattie turned to the mirror and saw the creature had been joined by two others, all of them grinning with rows and rows of sharp, tiny teeth.

"Hattie, help!" screamed Isabel. The closet in the mirror slammed shut.

Hattie turned to look at the real closet. She ran and opened it. The space was full of shelves and towels and bottles of soap. There was no room for a person to stand inside, let alone four creatures.

Hattie ran to her bedroom and shut the door. She collapsed onto her bed and sobbed. It was a dream. It had to be. How could Isabel disappear inside a mirror? What were those horrible little things with the yellow eyes and the cruel smiles?

Hattie heard a creak.

She lifted her wet eyes from her pillow and watched as the closet door across her bedroom slowly opened. A scaly pink hand reached around the edge of the door. It was followed by a familiar looking face.

Isabel?

The strange creature looked like Hattie's sister, but with pink, scaly skin and yellow eyes. She looked at Hattie, opened her toothy mouth and said, "Your turn, Hattie. You can come in now."

LEGENDS

—

TRUE OR FALSE

Tynan hated Language Arts tests, especially on Friday afternoons. But Mr. Loup's tests were usually pretty easy. Tynan grabbed his pencil and started reading.

This test will concentrate on the important monsters from our Legends unit.

Duh, thought Tynan.

1. Monsters are based on real, living creatures.

True or False

Um, that wasn't so easy. Dragons were not based on living creatures, but things like zombies were. Their legends came from real life — people who had been accidentally buried. People who had fainted or something like that, and then woke up and found themselves in a coffin and climbed out. The lucky ones did, anyway. Tynan circled *True*.

2. Monsters are a symbol
   of our fears about the
   unknown.

   True or False

Tynan had no idea what that question meant. He figured it sounded smart, so he'd better answer *True*.

3. Shape-shifters are
   a type of legendary
   monster.

   True or False

Shape-shifters were creepy dudes, Tynan remembered. Some of the old Viking warriors would wear the skins of animals they had killed. Then they turned into those same animals. Like bears or wolves. Tynan had once

watched his uncle skin a bear he had shot.
It looked cool, but Tynan couldn't imagine
putting a bloody carcass around his shoulders.
Gross. And the smell! Tynan circled *True*.

4. Shape-shifters can
   disguise themselves as
   human beings.

   True or False

Easy one, thought Tynan. *True.* Ty looked up
at Mr. Loup standing in the corner. His teacher
was watching the clock. He probably wanted to
start the weekend just as badly as his students
did.

5. Your teacher is a shape-
   shifter.

   True or False

Tynan looked up again. Was Mr. Loup
smiling? It was one of his typical trick
questions. Very funny. But as Tynan pretended
to study the test, he watched under lowered
eyebrows. He thought the man's smile changed.
It looked wider. He could see Mr. Loup's teeth.

He'd circle *True* just for kicks. Mr. Loup
would find it funny.

6. If your teacher were
   a shape-shifter, he
   would survive by eating
   humans.

   True or False

Ha ha! Totally gross, thought Tynan. But true.
A werewolf was a kind of shape-shifter, and
they ate humans.

7. With so many humans to
   eat in one classroom,
   a good method would be
   alphabetical order.

   True or False

Tynan heard his classmates shifting in their
chairs. A few people snickered. Jill, the class
nerd, gasped. Mr. Loup was still smiling. Tynan
frowned at the question. If it *was* true, he was
glad his last name was Zimmerman.

8. You wish your last name
   came at the end of the
   alphabet.

   True or False

Tynan blinked. He looked up quickly and met Mr. Loup's gaze. The teacher was smiling. He was also nodding slightly, as if he could read Tynan's mind.

A cold shudder ran down Tynan's body. What if that question was only on *his* test? What if the tests had been written specially for each student? Suddenly, Tynan felt like he needed to use the restroom. He was about to raise his hand, but he couldn't move. His feet were glued to the floor. His bottom was stuck to the chair.

Tynan's pal Kent shouted, "What's going on?"

Tynan looked quickly down at the next question.

> 9. Shape-shifters
>   hypnotize their
>   victims before they
>   attack.
>
> True or False

That's what it is, he thought. *A joke.* Mr. Loup was pranking them. Somehow he had hypnotized the entire class. That's why he had been holding that funny little crystal he kept on his desk. The sunlight from the window glittered on the crystal as Mr. Loup turned it over and over in his hand.

Tynan wanted to laugh. No sound came from his throat. He tried to ask a question, but he couldn't speak.

As he stared at his teacher, he thought he heard the man's voice in his head. *Aren't you glad the test is almost over?* Tynan looked down at the paper.

10. You are glad the test
    is almost over.

True or False

For the students whose last names begin with A through G, you may now put your pencils down and follow me.

Tynan and half the other students were still frozen. They watched as their classmates at the front of the room slowly stood up and followed Mr. Loup toward the window. He opened it in one swift move. He swung his legs over the sill. The students followed, one by one. In a few moments they had disappeared into the woods next to the school.

A wolf's howl echoed in the distance.

Tynan and the others all dropped their pens at the same time. They could move again.

Another howl came from the woods. Jill looked at Tynan with fear in her eyes. "Do you think this means we can skip the bonus question?" she asked.

THE
LIBRARY
CLAW

Darren didn't realize the town library had a second hidden library inside it. Not until he had to go there and rescue someone.

In fact, he rarely went inside the building, though it was hard to miss. It sat in the center of Ravenville, like a spider at the center of its web. The huge, sprawling, three-story pile of brick and stone was more than two hundred years old.

Over the years, the townspeople added rooms, wings, turrets, fireplaces, and staircases to it until the library that Darren knew covered an entire city block.

He trudged up the stone stairs to the entrance. He had only two days left to turn in a report for history class. He hadn't even started working on it. He had to write about a person who lived in Ravenville during the 1800s.

Boring, thought Darren.

Inside the library's main entrance, Darren got a surprise. His heart began pounding so hard he was afraid people might hear it.

He had caught a glimpse of his classmate, Dawn Potter. Dawn Potter, the prettiest girl he had ever spoken to. He hadn't said a lot to her. He'd only said, "It's page twenty-six," when Dawn had asked what page number the teacher was talking about once. But he put as much feeling into those three words as he could possibly muster.

She's working on the same assignment, Darren thought. *Maybe I should ask her about her report, or where she got her information.* That would give him an excuse to talk to her. Darren watched Dawn join two girls at a table in one of the reading rooms. *Great! There goes my chance,* he thought. He couldn't talk to her with the other girls around.

Darren wandered around the huge building. He climbed stairs, explored hallways, and looked at the endless stacks of books. He was hunting for the biography section.

At an information desk, he found a librarian, a young guy wearing retro glasses and a preppy sweatshirt. When Darren asked about biographies, the guy asked if he was looking for something more specific.

"Yeah," said Darren. "Someone who lived in town. And they had to live in the 1800s."

A gleam appeared in the man's eyes. "Really? In Ravenville?"

That's what Darren had said.

"Oh, this will be cool," said the librarian, coming around his desk. "Follow me."

Darren had no idea how enormous the library was. He lost count of the hallways and staircases. How far was Mr. Librarian taking him?

When they had gone down several flights of steps, the librarian stopped at a blank wall. It was paneled in smooth honey-colored wood.

Darren said, "It's a wall."

The librarian smiled and shook his head. He put his hands against the wall and pushed. A hidden door swung inward. Darren could see rays of dusty sunlight trying to penetrate the gloom. The guy took a few steps forward, gesturing toward the dimness.

Walking farther in, Darren saw a tall room filled floor-to-ceiling with rows and rows of shelves. Hundreds, probably of thousands, of old books filled the shelves. Piles of ancient volumes lay scattered on the floor like miniature pyramids.

"I believe, *this* is the biography section you're looking for," said the librarian. "These are all biographies of people who settled or lived in Ravenville from 1790 to 1880. This is the perfect place for you."

"Where exactly are we?" asked Darren.

"The library, of course." He hesitated. "But this is part of the Inner Library. Very old, very old. Not many people come down here anymore. It's reserved for our . . . *special* patrons." He turned away and walked toward the exit. "I'll leave the door open," he added.

"Uh, thanks," said Darren, but when he turned around, the librarian was already gone.

Darren found that the rows were labeled by year. It shouldn't be too hard to find someone from the right time period. He walked in and out of shadows, working his way farther into the maze.

One section intrigued him. It was next to one of the walls, and was closed off by a musty velvet rope. It was easy enough to step over. Darren scanned the books. They were ancient, all right. Probably about the oldest people who had lived in the town. Darren was struck by how thin they all were. *Good, not too much to read,* he thought. He noticed that instead of titles, names were printed along the spines. *Becker . . . Biltmore . . . Brannigan . . .*

One's as good as another, thought Darren.

He reached for a book, and then stopped. Out of the corner of his eye he saw a shadow. A shape passed swiftly at the end of the row. "Is someone else here?" he called. When there was no answer, Darren walked to the end of the row, leaned over the velvet rope, and glanced in each direction. No one.

He went back to the shelf and grabbed a book. It didn't have a title. Darren held the book in both hands. Something moved. He heard what he thought was breathing. In and out. In and out. With each breath, the book seemed to pulse in his hands. The boy carefully opened it.

He cried out in surprise.

On one of the pages was a picture of Dawn.

It wasn't drawn or painted on. It was a photograph. Underneath he saw two dates written in blood red. One was her birth date, and the other the date she would die. It was today's date.

This has to be a joke, thought Darren.

He marked the page with his thumb and flipped through the rest of the book. More photos, more people, and all of them had the dates of their deaths. Some were today, some tomorrow or next week.

Wait! There was his sister, Lenore. Her death would be next month, according to the book. But how? Lenore wasn't sick. She was only six years old. What was going on?

Darren looked back at the photo of Dawn. It had changed. Her skin looked paler, more wrinkled. Her hair wasn't as shiny as it normally was.

He closed the book and shivered. Now it had a title: RECIPES FOR THE BEAST.

A shadow fell across the book. Darren looked up quickly. Something had momentarily blocked out the light from one of the high windows. The shadow again. It was closer this time.

Darren didn't care about putting the book back on the shelf. He leaped over the velvet rope. He raced down row after row. When he reached the door, he stopped to catch his breath.

The people who die in that book, he thought. *Was something going to eat them?*

Darren heard a cry.

He ignored the door. He followed the cries. They grew louder as he neared the center of the hidden library. Turning a corner, he spied a girl lying on the floor.

Had she fallen and hurt herself? She was clawing at the carpet. Her feet were stuck inside the lowest shelf of a bookcase. The girl screamed again and moved backward, as if being pulled into the shelf.

Her eyes hunted desperately for something to grip. She saw Darren's shoe and looked up. It was Dawn Potter.

"Please," she said.

A growl shook the room. Dawn cried out, and Darren reached down and grabbed her hands. He pulled, but whatever was pulling from the other side was strong.

"Don't let go!" she yelled.

Darren looked at the shelf. A claw at the end of a thick, scaly arm was gripping Dawn's foot. Darren knew it was the beast.

He heard a giggle. The librarian was standing behind him. He pushed his glasses farther up the bridge of his nose and laughed again. "Looks like she'll become part of our permanent collection," he said.

"Help us," said Darren.

"You can't escape that thing," said the librarian. "But don't worry. You can always visit her here in the biographies. She'll make a beautiful addition."

Darren was so angry he released his hold and swung at the guy. He hit him square in the face, sending his glasses flying. The librarian fell to the floor. He gave Darren an evil look. "You're next," he said.

A scaly hand reached out from the low shelf. The claw gripped the man by his hair and began pulling him in. He screamed, louder than Darren thought a person could scream.

"Hurry," said Dawn.

Darren reached down and pulled her to her feet.

The librarian's head had disappeared into the shelf. His legs were kicking wildly. Another growl shook the room, and the man's legs were pulled into the shadows. He was gone.

"Come on," said Darren.

The two ran out of the hidden library. They pulled the wooden door shut behind them and rushed up the stairs to the main floor.

"Are you all right?" Darren asked. They stopped at the top of the steps.

"I don't know," said Dawn. "Maybe."

Patrons wandered around them, gazing into open books or glancing at shelves. Students sat at tables with their homework in front of them. Sunlight streamed through the narrow windows. Everything looked normal.

Dawn was catching her breath. "I think . . . ," she began, "I think I'm getting an *F* on this assignment."

"Me too," said Darren. "I don't think I could read a book now about someone who was dead."

"Yeah," Dawn agreed. She tried to smile, but Darren felt certain she was going to cry. "I'll — I'll see you at school," she stammered. Then she hurried away.

Darren hadn't told her about the book. The one with her photograph. But things were OK now, right? They had defied the book. Dawn was alive and not dinner for some unknown beast.

Darren felt drained of energy. He needed to get home. He needed to find a place where he wasn't surrounded by books. He walked quickly to the main door of the library. He was reaching for the handle when someone ahead of him opened it for him.

"Thanks," Darren said. It was the librarian!

The man pushed his glasses higher on his nose and smiled. "Librarians don't really go away," he said. "They're always *bound* to come back."

He giggled as Darren ran down the stone steps.

MICHAEL DAHL TELLS ALL

William Shakespeare, my favorite non-scary-story writer, once asked, "Where is Fancy bred?" That was his way of saying how does our imagination (our "Fancy") come up with its ideas? Even he wasn't sure. Shakespeare was, however, inspired by his friends, by books and poems he had read, and by plays he had seen. Same for me, though I've seen more TV and movies than plays. On the following pages, I've tried to recall where I got the ideas for the stories in this book.

SECTION 1: IS ANYONE HOME?

THE BOY IN THE BASEMENT

Basements and attics make me nervous. They are the extreme ends of a house, where extreme things might happen. My aunt used to live in a house where the basement was busy with ghostly activity — unexplained footsteps and voices, hands that reached out of nowhere to close doors, unseen things that growled. I told my brain that I needed to come up with a super scary story for the book, and this one popped into my brain. The creepy elements are all there: ghostly children, mysterious messages, noises in the night, and, of course, the basement.

SKIPPY

I recently watched a YouTube video of Japanese robots that look frighteningly human. It's only a matter of time before we start creating robotic animals, before digital dogs and cats will be available at the local pet store. How long will it be before something else small and innocent is built in a factory somewhere?

SHADOW SHOES

Two of my favorite comic-book heroes were
Invisible Kid and Phantom Girl. They had the
powers I always wanted: to turn invisible and
walk through walls. Imagine what you'd see and
hear. All secret stuff, mostly. You could hear what
your friends or parents said when you weren't
around. You could walk inside locked places like
bank vaults or prisons or zoo cages and have cool
adventures. Of course, something would probably
go wrong. After all, superpowers and magical
objects come with rules, and those rules should
not be broken. Ask Harry Potter. Or Phantom
Girl. Or poor Daphne in this story. I got the name
Daphne from a Greek myth about a young girl
who turns into, what else? A tree.

THE WAITING POOL

I had a wading pool as a kid, and my friends and
I enjoyed many hours playing in it during the
summer. One of my favorite things to do as an
author is to take something seemingly innocent,
like a kids' pool, and turn it into something
terrifying. I was also thinking of the legendary
"Fountain of Youth," a pool that magically washes
away the years of older people who swim in it or
drink its water. Well, what if I combined those
two things, and then twisted it? What if the water
made you really, really old?

FLUSHED

All those poor, dead goldfish. They don't even get a decent backyard burial like a cat or a dog. Just a flush! Here's another story where I turned a normal, everyday event on its head. Besides, wouldn't a huge goldfish look intimidating?

THE BABY MONITOR

This is one of those ideas that just popped into my head when I saw a picture of a baby monitor online. What if the baby monitor was actually a baby? Babies are scary creatures. They crawl, they slobber, they eat whatever they find lying around, and they scream. That could easily describe an alien monster. Later, I dreamed a baby was walking toward my bedroom in the middle of the night. I woke up, totally creeped out, wrote it all down in a notepad, and finished the story the next day.

THE TALL AND SLENDER MAN

This is my addition to the Slender Man urban legend. I decided to make him the messenger of bad news. Whether he causes bad things to happen, or simply warns people about them is left up in the air. You as a reader can decide. I have a friend with a pup named Kenji, so that's where the dog's name came from.

DONT READ THIS STORY AT MIDNIGHT!

I like stories that have warnings as titles. And I have never gotten over the idea that there is something under my bed at night. Even as an adult, I think about what could be down there. An alligator? A zombie? Something worse?

BIG FURRY

The cellar in this story is based on several different basements I've been down in, including the one in my aunt's old place that used to be a boarding house for loggers in the middle of northern Minnesota. My aunt had a black fur coat that hung on a hook just inside the basement door. No matter how many times I'd seen it before, that furry mass always looked like a monster to me. Or one of the hungry black bears that roam the snowy woods of Minnesota.

SECTION 2: GOING SOMEWHERE?

FINGERS ON THE GLASS

This story has been pinging around my brain for a long time. As a kid, riding in the backseat of the car at night, before video games and phone apps, I often stared out the dark windows. I imagined all kinds of things out there. Things that were just out of sight . . . perhaps on the roof or the trunk of the car. In sixth grade, my cousins and I watched a classic *Twilight Zone* episode about a gremlin on the wing of the airplane. Yikes! That show not only scared me even more about flying, but it gave me a healthy respect for what's on the other side of windows. Especially windows on moving vehicles. Now that I've gotten this story out of my head and written down, I hope dark windows won't bother me so much.

THE DARKEST BRIDGE

Can we all agree that bridges are just plain scary? I've always been afraid of them. Recently I read a book about "crybaby bridges." These are supposedly haunted bridges, the sites of tragic car accidents where, as a result, the spirits of the dead can still be heard crying at night. Sounds like a story to me!

THE PHANTOM TRAIN

The story of a ghostly train has been pinging around in my brain for a long time. When I was younger, our backyard ended at the railroad tracks. Watching the trains roaring by, day and night, became a part of growing up. One summer, there was a horrible accident at the train crossing a block from our house. A car had smashed into the side of a moving train. The kids of the neighborhood all gathered to survey the wreck. I'll never forget seeing only half a car sitting there on the road. The other half, with the driver, was gone. My imagination produced terrible images of what the driver would look like. I guess those images never left my brain.

NIGHT OF THE FALLING STAR

My mother saw a meteor one morning. She saw it crash in the field beyond the train tracks that bordered our yard. She said it had colorful lights all around its edge too. My friends and I knew what it really was. A UFO! That afternoon, we hiked across the tracks and investigated the field. No meteor, but we did find a large round imprint in the ground. Grass grew around the edges of it, but nothing grew inside. What had my mother really seen that morning? Ever since then, I've wanted to write a story about kids who encounter a meteor. But would the rock from outer space be radioactive? Would it have a weird effect on people who got too close? Maybe it's a good thing my friends and I didn't find anything on the other side of the tracks.

THE GIRL IN THE GRAVEYARD

What goes around comes around. Karma. Do something good and it will come back to you. But do something bad . . . look out! That's the point of this story. A bad deed, even something minor like pranking a sister or a friend, will create another bad deed that will bounce back at you. I thought a graveyard would be the perfect setting for Bradley to meet his destiny. A destiny that involves an unliving person. I say "unliving" because dolls, strictly speaking, aren't dead, since they're not alive in the first place. Or are they?

STUCK

Spiders don't bother me, but their webs sure do. Hate 'em. I really don't like how they feel against my face when I run into one. I park my car in the garage, and there must be a whole family of spiders living in there. Once, I left the window in the car open overnight, and the next morning a web was already stretching across the dashboard. Those little monsters are fast. Imagine what a giant-sized one could do.

THE NIGHT OCTOPUS

One of the coolest things your imagination does is make you see two things at the same time. You look at a weird shape in the bark of a tree and you see a face. You look at a small cloud and see a flying saucer. Or you look at curtains waving in the wind, as I did as a small child, and you see them as a living creature . . . with tentacles.

THE HORNLOCK

This little tale has such a spooky origin that I can't even tell you the whole story. Just know that a friend of mine, when she was young, had an imaginary friend who may not have been so . . . imaginary. That imaginary friend's name was very similar to Hornlock. Second, my brother-in-law, Larry, used to sleep out on the porch in summer as a kid, and he very often had nightmares out there, all alone. I smooshed those ideas together to create this story. Whenever I re-read it, it still gives me shivers.

SECTION 3: WATCH OUT!

MEMBER OF THE BAND

My elementary school had several murals in its hallways. I sometimes pretended the painted figures of the students and animals came to life, jumping down to the floor and running into the classrooms. The idea for this story started with the opposite view: What if a living, breathing student became part of the mural? What would it feel like to be flat and part of a wall? Would a mural have its own separate world? How frightening to know that you'd have to stay up there until it was your turn again to be real, until everyone else had their chance.

THE HUNGRY SNOWMAN

I read a lot of science fiction (sci-fi), including old sci-fi comics. One of the comics I've collected has an outrageously bonkers cover. It shows evil alien snowmen invading Earth, shooting death rays from their eyes. So cool. I happened to see this one again while hunting for something to read, and it got me thinking. Not all snowmen are Frosty. And if a snowman did come to life, what would it eat? Something that's easy to reach, I figured, something close at hand!

THE BALLOON

Balloons seem harmless, which is why I wanted
to use one in a scary tale. Authors like doing that,
"topsy-turvying" people or objects or events that
seem normal and innocent. Also, years ago when
I was quite young, my dad and I would watch
The Prisoner on TV. It was a weird adventure/
spy/science fiction show about prisoners of
a seemingly quiet seaside town. If any of the
prisoners tried to escape, however, a strange
white balloon came out of nowhere and tracked
them down. I guess I've never forgotten that
unnerving white sphere bouncing along the shore,
chasing some poor guy until . . .

A HAND IN THE DARK

I'm a big fan of old-time science fiction movies.
I watched them as a kid, and I particularly liked
the ones where a science experiment goes wrong
and creates a monster. The creepiest monsters
are the ones that look like goo or tar. They ooze
under doors and drip down stairs to attack their
victims. I figured a good place for a monster
to attack would be one of those eerily isolated
movie theaters at the end of a super-long hallway.
Because if you did hear something weird, you'd
think it was coming from the screen, right? Not
from the creature sitting next to you. (This is one
reason I never go to the movies alone!)

THE WIZARD OF AAAAAHHHHHS!

Our junior high put on a production of *The Wizard of Oz*, and practically the entire seventh grade was cast. Although I was only a general in Emerald City, it was still exciting to be a part of the show. But the rehearsals were long and tiring. Many late nights, my friends and I walked from the dressing room through dark, deserted hallways toward the exit. The backstage of a theater, when all the actors and crew have left, is an eerie, silent place. I used to wonder, if you were alone back there and listened closely, would you hear echoes of shows from long ago? Would you see shadowy figures in costumes glide across the stage?

LITTLE IMPS

Mirrors fascinate me. After I read *Alice Through the Looking Glass* in fourth grade, I tried climbing through various mirrors in my house. Just so you know, it didn't work. Despite my failures, I was sure there was another world on the other side. I still am sure; the trick is how to get there. This tale, besides tying in my thing for mirrors, also includes a term thrown at my childhood friends and me by some of the neighborhood grown-ups. "Little imps!" We were too noisy, too boisterous, and having too much fun. But "imp" has another meaning, as the sisters discover in this story.

LEGENDS - TRUE OR FALSE

This story started as a challenge I gave myself. Could I write a scary tale that would be in the form of an exam? A test in English class? Tests are only scary if you don't know the answers, right? But what if it's even more frightening when you *do* know the answers? I hadn't written a werewolf story in a long time either, so somehow that got in the mix, too.

THE LIBRARY CLAW

Many creatures feed on old books: paper louses, brown moths, black carpet beetles. What if a similar creature had an unending supply of food in a damp, dark section of a library? How big would it grow? How powerful would it become? The deathwatch beetle can tunnel through a book fifty times its size. I imagined that the bigger one of those tiny gluttons became, the bigger the food they would require. I based the librarian on Batman's foe, the Riddler. He seems like a kooky, spooky, unpredictable character that would giggle, appear suddenly out of thin air, and hide out in a place full of words. Words and stories never die. Perhaps those who live off them are also immortal.

ABOUT THE AUTHOR

Michael Dahl, the author of the Library of Doom and Troll Hunters series, is an expert on fear. He is afraid of heights (but he still flies). He is afraid of small, enclosed spaces (but his house is crammed with over 3,000 books). He is afraid of ghosts (but that same house is haunted). He hopes that by writing about fear, he will eventually be able to overcome his own. So far it is not working. But he is afraid to stop. He claims that, if he had to, he would travel to Mount Doom in order to toss in a dangerous piece of jewelry. Even though he is afraid of volcanoes. And jewelry.

ABOUT THE ILLUSTRATOR

Xavier Bonet is an illustrator and comic-book artist who resides in Barcelona. Experienced in 2D illustration, he has worked as an animator and a background artist for several different production companies. He aims to create works full of color, texture, and sensation, using both traditional and digital tools. His work in children's literature is inspired by magic and fantasy as well as his passion for the art.